Jackie's
JOURNEY

La Patron's Den
Book One

La Patron's Den: Jackie's Journey, Book One

Sydney Addae
Copyright 2017 by Addae, Sydney
ISBN: 978-1-937334-82-6
First Edition Electronic March 2017
Published by Sydney Addae

Jackie's Journey

When you grow up in a quasi-military compound with the knowledge that the walls and security are in place to keep you safe from your father's enemies, you dream of a day when you escape those walls.

When you grow up learning the importance and infallibility of pack, your life can take a dramatic turn when you see a different reality.

When you grow up in a stable, loving home, with family who love and will fight to the death for you, it emboldens you to live your life on your terms.

La Patron's Den is a series about Silas and Jasmine Knight's four pups: Jackie, Adam, Renee and David. Each book tells their stories as young adults embarking on new chapters of their lives.

Jackie's Journey

Jackie accepts a job in corporate America and quickly learns the difference between working with humans and pack. Disillusioned she searches for something that interests and challenges her before accepting her sister's advice to return to the Wolf Nation to work. Join Jackie on her journey of inner discovery and the realization that the world is not the way she imagined it to be.

This is the first book in the La Patron's Den Series.

Thanks to my Facebook group, La Patron's Den. This book celebrates all we've been through together for the past four years. Thanks for your support. Thanks to Michelle and Vicky, two great Admins. Also thanks to Vicky Z., Karen M., Sally R., Trisin C. for your continued support in the Nation.

Thanks

Sydney

CHAPTER ONE

"Last quarter we surpassed corporate projections," Smith the marketing director said in the department heads board meeting.

"Not really," Mr. Bradley, president of the company said looking across the table at Jackie. "Ms. Knight's changes in the way we positioned ourselves clearly pointed to the gains we made. Her accurate models led us to this point."

"It was a team effort," Jackie said, as heat rose to her face from the sudden attention drawn to her. In the past few months she learned corporation mentality wasn't like pack. Success wasn't celebrated throughout the halls of industry, nor did it directly benefit everyone.

Mr. Bradley waved his hand. "Yes, of course. It was your team who recognized the niche that changed the direction of the marketing campaign." He nodded, congratulating himself for taking the risk and implementing her ideas over a much more experienced marketing team. That hadn't made her any friends.

"Go on, Smith," Mr. Bradley said with a smug grin. The older man reminded her of Jacques, her grandfather and her father's closest friend with his salt and pepper hair, and mild disposition.

"That's about it. Everyone has the numbers in front of them. Overall, we're on track for another successful quarter, sales are up 20%." He sat back in his seat and looked around the table.

As the only junior executive in the meeting, Jackie didn't say anything but watched the interaction around the table. Mr. Bradley took over and presented his points. Then Mr. Johnson, a senior vice-president spoke. Kristin Scott, the only other female in the room, remained quiet while taking notes on her tablet.

Overall, Jackie would have preferred skipping this meeting. But Mr. Bradley seemed determined to keep her front and center since he personally recruited her from a Department of Defense internship where she'd been on the winning team of a strategic competition to solve an economic task. With a background in finance, business, economics, and sociology, her father deemed her overqualified for this position. But she jumped at the chance to work in corporate America.

When the meeting dismissed, Mr. Bradley singled her out to walk with him.

"I'm very proud of the job you've done so far. Do you need anything?" he asked.

Considering she worked in an office barely large enough to move around she wondered if she should ask for more space. But since most junior executives used cubicles, she remained silent on that score. "No, Sir, everything's good," she said noticing eyes on them as they moved down the corridor.

"Good. Good." Lowering his voice, he leaned close. "I have a project I want you to look at, give me some feedback. Nothing formal, just want your take on it," he said stopping in the middle of the hall, causing people to walk around them.

"Yes, Sir." She hoped it wasn't another acquisition. Last week he'd asked her opinion on a company that would require more to turn around than the packet proposed. When she'd pointed out what seemed logical to her, he claimed she had stopped the company from making a huge mistake.

Turning she left for her office.

"At least Bradley's new wonder child has a nice ass," someone whispered behind her back.

Jackie's jaw tightened but she didn't turn to see who'd made the remark. When she arrived nine months ago, and heard the first sordid whisper, it cut her to the core. She didn't understand why people made ridiculous assumptions. Once she learned jealousy ran rampant amongst co-workers and nothing she did would change their nature, she stopped caring. Closing the door to her office, she released a long breath. Working with humans was nothing like pack. Instead of being happy and supportive when her idea made the company money, the very ones she worked alongside every day stopped speaking or inviting her to join them after work.

What're you doing?" Renee her sister asked through their mental link. One of a quad, Jackie, her sister Renee, and her two brothers, Adam and David, had a strong mental connection and spoke to each other through mental links since they were toddlers.

Just got out of a meeting."

Boring," Renee said.

"Yeah, it was." She paused. *Humans are weird."*

Mom's human." Renee said. *So is Aunt Renee and Grandma."*

Twirling a long strand of her inky black hair, Jackie sat in her chair and spun around to face the wall. *"Obviously, not all of them, maybe just the ones in Houston."*

I doubt Houston has a monopoly on selfishness."

Jackie agreed. *"What's going on?"* She and Renee talked every day while they both were at work. She looked forward to their conversations; it kept her from being homesick. Plus, she hadn't made any new friends here in the local pack. Being the daughter of the top Alpha in the country, La Patron, worked like a pesticide, and kept people away.

"Adam and Tomas are heading to Rome this weekend. Dad agreed he could go and play soccer with the European league. He's stoked. Matt and Davian are throwing Tomas a party to send him off."

Awesome. He didn't tell me he made the team." Jackie wondered how Renee felt about her ex-boyfriend leaving the country. Tomas had professed his love to Renee but she, all of them, wanted the same kind of relationship their parents La Patron and Jasmine, had. They all decided to wait for their mates. No one knew the exact age or time when mates recognized each other, which put a hold on Tomas and Renee relationship from going further.

Her older brothers, and Thorne, her sister-in-law's brother met their mates in their twenties. Thorne told his sister, he and his mate hadn't immediately recognized each other. It took a couple weeks before they knew, which wasn't the case with her father or older brothers. Research on half-breeds was ongoing. There were so many variables that created anomalies.

Adam's going over their contracts and making sure everything's above board. Daddy's helping him find a place to stay with good security, 'Renee said

How much security is going with him? 'Jackie asked thinking of Tango, her personal security guard chosen by Theron, the Alpha of Texas, from his personal security staff. Jackie was sure there were others watching nearby but Tango was her point of contact.

"*One, I think. Adam's thoughts are scrambled right now, be glad you aren't listening in. David shut him out, telling him to get it together.*"

Jackie smiled. David was the fourth in their quad and the easiest going of the four of them. She missed her brothers and sister but her determination to find her place in the world and make a difference took her outside the Wolf Nation. "*I'm happy for him... and Tomas. You okay?*"

Yeah. I made peace with the idea we may not be mates and so did he. This is a good move for him, for both of us. I'll miss him, but who knows? The next time we see each other things may be different. 'Renee paused. "*Are you ready to give up your quest of helping humans?*"

Jackie smiled. *I'm human, Mama's just as much a part of me as Daddy.*"

True but we don't have much experience dealing with our human nature. Is it hard?"

Yes, because we were raised with the one for all mentality. Pack protects, provides and nurtures pack. Nobody's hungry, cold or naked. Out here, maybe it's because there are so many, they don't look out for each other. 'She thought of the halfway house and other charities she supported financially. *Some do, but not enough. They aren't taught benevolence as children and it shows when they become adults.*"

Every time I ask that question, I keep hoping for a different answer."

Me too, that's why I don't mind you asking. It helps keep me grounded. I want to make a difference," Jackie said.

In somebody's bank account?" Renee asked in a dry tone.

Jackie winced. *"Before you go off on my choice of working in a corporation again, remember I interned for three years with Cain and Abel at the Pentagon as a military strategist. By the time I graduated I wanted something different."*

Different you got," Renee muttered. *"Still can't believe Mama talked Daddy into letting you take the job. I think it had a domino effect. Nionis moved to Knoxville to work and Pierre moved to Charleston, started his own business."*

Really? I hadn't heard." Nionis and Pierre's father, Cameron, was Alpha of West Virginia and her dad's godson. Cameron and his mate, Lilly, adopted seven pups and gave birth to another four. Academically brilliant, Pierre had been in a wheelchair as long as she knew him. For him to move out was major. *"What's Nionis doing?"*

Something to do with teaching, I'm not sure. We aren't as close as the two of you. She left last week, I just found out today when Mama told Cameron about Adam."

I'll call Mama tonight," Jackie said suddenly wanting to hear her mom's voice again.

It would be awesome if we could mind-link with her," Renee said.

Since they had discussed their inability to link with their mother several times since leaving home for college, and it never changed, Jackie didn't have much to say about it. As a human breeder, their mom mind linked with two people, their father and Asia, her best friend.

"*Yeah.*" Jackie spun around at the tap on her door. *Someone's here, hold tight,"* she told Renee.

"Come in," she said inhaling and then wrinkled her nose as the door opened.

"Got a minute?" Kristin Cross, a senior marketing manager asked as she stepped inside, closing the door behind her.

"Sure," Jackie said waving to one of the chairs in front of her desk. *Cross is back. Wonder what game she's playing today,"* she told Renee.

What color is she wearing?" Renee asked.

"Red jacket, black skirt," Jackie told Renee while waiting for Kristin to speak.

"First let me say how happy I am to have someone with your education and abilities on our team. You made us all look really good this morning in the meeting. As the only other female on the executive board, I appreciate it. Especially with you being so young." She shook her head.

Power colors," Renee said. *I'm sure you have on some sort of blue."*

Blue dress. She played the woman card and then hit me with being too young," Jackie told her sister. *Deceit's rolling off her in waves."*

What does she want?" Renee asked.

"Thank you," Jackie said politely.

"Mr. Bradley has several projects he's been looking at." Kristin looked at Jackie. "Last week you gave your opinion on one of them. May I ask what barometers you based your decision?"

"Excuse me?" Kristin had to know she was out of line asking about Mr. Bradley's project.

The older woman's nostril's flared and Jackie realized just how much the woman disliked her. Leaning back, she watched as Kristin pulled it together.

"We, my staff and I, worked countless hours on that project. It seemed solid, yet Bradley rejected it. I just learned he did it because of your report." She rubbed her hand against her skirt and crossed her leg. "You can imagine I'm confused what you saw that we missed."

Jackie told Renee what Kristin said while clicking keys on her keyboard.

Haters hate. If you can tell her without getting in trouble, go ahead. You're there to make the world a better place. Start with her," Renee said.

"Should I ask Mr. Bradley first?" Jackie asked Kristin ignoring Renee's advice. "From time to time he has me look over sensitive material and I'm not sure what I'm allowed to share."

Kristin's gaze locked with Jackie's for a brief moment and she realized she had just made an enemy. Damn. Drama wasn't why she decided to leave the Pentagon and do this kind of work.

"I came to you as a co-worker trying to learn, but I see you're not the team player I thought you were," Kristin said, her eyes hard. "I'm sure Mr. Bradley will apprise me of the problem with that project eventually, but..." She stood and pointed at Jackie. "We lost a good man because that project's been canceled. He had a family, a daughter around your age in college. Think about that while sitting in this office."

"Why would I think about someone I don't know?" Resentment flowed through Jackie. "If my findings in the project were wrong, Mr. Bradley would've taken it to the next step. Don't blame me for doing my job --"

"Killing my projects is not your job," Kristin said stiffly. "You're here to work on marketing strategies. Not review complicated business plans that have been signed off with people with higher degrees and more experience than you could ever accomplish."

Anger flared in her chest. Clenching and unclenching her hand, she held Kristin's gaze until the woman looked away. A few moments later, Jackie wrote the problem she found in the canceled project on a piece of paper and slid it across the desk. "That's what I found."

Kristin snatched up the paper and read it. Several expressions flew across her face, the last being shock. "How'd you come up with this?"

"Give it to those higher minds to figure out," Jackie snapped as she pointed at the woman. "Don't ever tell me who I am or what I can or cannot do. You don't know me at all. That's a one-time gift, take your fake smiles and false words and get out of here. If you ask me anything like this again I will refuse to review the next project for Mr. Bradley and tell him you're the reason why."

Kristin's jaw tightened but a flash of admiration chased by fear rolled through her gaze. "You're golden right now, but you'll mess up soon. Pretty things like you always do."

Tired of being nice, Jackie stood and sat on the corner of her desk bringing their gazes even. "Haters hate. Do your job, I'll do mine. The day that changes is the day I walk out the door, head high to the next assignment. I've given you what you came for, now get the hell out of here."

"Gutsy," Kristin nodded and left taking the paper with her.

She's gone, Jackie told Renee.

You gave it to her?"

Yep. She filled her sister in on the rest of the conversation.

Why do you put up with that stuff? Renee asked. *"Come home, or go back to Maryland, work with Cain or Rone, or Rese or anywhere in the pack you want. You have options."*

Jackie looked at her watch, it was lunchtime. Grabbing her purse, she left her office. Several of the women and a few men turned away as she walked by. Whispers flowed regarding her meeting with the Dragon, their name for Kristin. Jackie was surprised how many thought better of her after that confrontation.

Weird.

She went across the street to a small local restaurant that served the best cuts of steak. She ate there three times a week. Human owned, the staff was nice and didn't hover. She took a seat in the back. If anyone asked if she was hiding, she'd say no. She just didn't want to be bothered.

We all have options, I'm exercising mine," she told Renee. *Daddy started the art museum for you and other pups with a passion for art. There's no reason for you to leave the Nation, you're making a difference already. I'm doing this for me."*

No reason for you to leave either, Renee muttered.

Jackie smiled, warmed by her sister's affection. The four of them were close and spoke daily but she and Renee had a special bond.

"I miss you too," Jackie said. *Get back to work, I'm at lunch."* She looked up and nodded at Tango who sat at a table up front.

Talk to you later," Renee said and disconnected.

Jackie ordered a medium rare steak, salad and lemonade. Taking out her phone she logged into a well-known head-hunting bulletin board to see if there were any new interesting jobs. Sure, she wanted to make a difference with her life, but Renee made a valid point. Making a few richer wasn't fulfilling. In fact, it was boring. The only reason she hadn't left after nine months was because her mom had gone to bat for her to try something new. It would suck big time to quit and admit she had been wrong. Although, knowing her mom, admitting humans were more different than just the cellular level could have been the reason she wanted Jackie to give corporate America a shot.

Nothing on the board piqued her interest. She set her phone aside when lunch was delivered. Halfway through her meal, she stopped eating and looked up. A tall, handsome man with dark hair slicked back from a widow's peak entered the restaurant, looked around and stared at her. Tango stood, ready to run interference.

Curious, Jackie watched him for a moment. In public, she kept her human side deeply emerged to keep her dual nature a secret to those who didn't already know she was La Patron's daughter. Every day she passed dual-natured beings without detection. The down side to keeping her beast submerged was it limited her ability to discern other dual-natureds through scent. Consequently, she relied on body cues, attitude and physical attributes all of which screamed this guy was a wolf. But he shouldn't be able to scent her at all.

Intrigued, she nodded. Tango stepped aside allowing the wolf to move toward her.

When he reached her table, he stopped and tipped his head in an abbreviated bow. "Hello, I am Jonas, may I sit and speak with you?"

Lunch was over in 10 minutes which may not be enough time. She hated rushing almost as much as starting and not finishing a task. "Not now, make an appointment with Tango to meet later." She held his gaze, until he nodded.

"Thank you, until we meet again." Turning, he walked toward Tango and sat at his table. Jackie watched them talk until she finished her meal. When the waiter returned, he took her plate and placed her paid meal receipt in front of her.

Frowning, she looked at him.

"The gentleman at the front table, not the regular one, the other, he paid for both meals and left a big tip, it's a good tip." With a huge grin, he walked off with her plates. Finished, Jackie left the table, nodded at Tango and Jonas as she left the restaurant wondering what Jonas wanted to discuss. Nothing came to mind. "I'll find out later."

When she returned to work, Mr. Bradley called her to his office. "I need to get another job, this is getting old," she thought on her way up to the executive suites.

"They're waiting for you," his personal assistant said nodding toward the door as she approached.

Inhaling at the door, Jackie rolled her eyes at the people waiting inside. Straightening her back, she entered with a smile of greeting. "Mr. Bradley, Ms. Cross, Mr. Johnson." She nodded at each and then at Mr. Bradley. "You wanted to see me?" Mr. Johnson, the company VP was a surprise but shouldn't have been. He was being groomed to take Mr. Bradley's place when he retired in a few years.

Bradley waved to the seat in at the small table. They all sat. "Kristin paid you a visit earlier, it was a test of sorts to see how you were getting along in the company. If you recall I asked you earlier if you had everything you needed, you said yes."

Jackie nodded. Kristin hadn't faked her dislike of Jackie, no matter what the woman said.

"You handled the situation admirably." He paused. "In the beginning. However, with pressure you gave her the information she requested."

Jackie nodded again, completely unfazed by anything he had to say. He'd recruited her, not the other way around.

They waited, as if she would explain. She returned his gaze and then looked at the other two, noticing satisfaction gleaming in Kristin's eyes.

"Sir?" Jackie said wanting to move this along.

Bradley cleared his throat. "Well, you weren't supposed to share that information with anyone."

"Not even a senior manager in my department who claimed she wanted the knowledge to do a better job in the future?" Jackie asked.

"Better job?" Johnson asked looking at Kristin.

"I told her my team worked on the project," Kristin said glancing at him.

"Marketing doesn't do acquisitions," Johnson said obviously forgetting Jackie worked in marketing and worked on an acquisition package.

Bradley frowned as he glanced at Kristin. "Tell us the conversation."

Jackie repeated, almost verbatim, the discussion but stopped at the threat of her downfall. It didn't matter, this wasn't her career but it was for the older woman.

"This sheds a different light on the situation, wouldn't you agree?" Johnson said sounding relieved.

"Indeed," Bradley said as he turned toward Jackie. "Thanks for clearing that matter, my assistant has that package for you on your way out. If I don't see you again today, enjoy your weekend."

For a split second, she thought of quitting rather than allow them to fire her on BS like this. But the idea of failing her first human job stopped the words in her throat. Instead, she said. "You too, Sir."

CHAPTER TWO

"Watch your feet or you'll get knocked on your..." Quinn
threw up his hands and then placed them on his waist, breathing
in meager dregs of patience as he watched the youngsters on the
mat. "Get up, both of you."

When the scout that his uncle used to search for broken
wolves brought these two, they were on the brink of dehydration,
malnourished and badly bruised. He'd kept them in the clinic in
the basement hooked to equipment for a day and a half. Rest
coupled with his limited cooking skills got them well enough for
physical testing.

The two boys scrambled to their feet and held their heads
down.

Their pitiful posture and expectation of some sort of
punishment stopped his rebuke and reminded him to tread gently.
"You're doing good." Their startled gazes pissed him off. He
tamped it down to get through this exercise.

"Half-breeds have always needed to be better than the others.
But..." he held up his finger snaring their attention. "We can do
things full-bloods don't and in some cases, can't do. That's how
we've survived. I'll teach you how to hide in plain sight. Fight to
keep your enemy at a disadvantage. It's not always the biggest or
strongest who wins the day." He tapped his forehead. "Every win

16

begins in here. Change how you see yourself. For years, someone lied and told you that you're worthless because of the circumstances of your birth." He shook his head, pleased they listened more intently.

"Uncle Ramos is almost 200 years old, one of the first half-breeds in this country. He taught me and hundred like me, how to survive against full-bloods."

"Aren't we supposed to be free? Why do we need to hide in full sight?" Alden, the red haired, 12 year old pup, asked.

Although disappointment rolled through him over the political climate in the Wolf Nation, Quinn gave his uncle approved response. "On paper half-breeds are free, even though rebels continue to hunt and kill us 20 years after La Patron's decree." He pointed at them. "Alphas can't be everywhere, rebels hide in the shadows killing half-breeds. By now you'd think the all-knowing La Patron would've wiped out all the rebels, yet they persist in destroying innocent lives." His uncle hadn't approved that last part.

Jude, a dark complexioned, 10-year-old pup, nodded and looked at Quinn. "It's mostly bad if you don't live with pack. They don't mess with them, just us who live on our land, separate. My sire tried to fight them but they were too many, by the time Alpha came they had taken me and my sister. Mam and Sire were dead, the farm on fire, crops destroyed. They took the animals, killed and ate them, but didn't feed us for days. Not 'til we agreed to join them."

Quinn's heart hurt. "How long ago was this?" Although he hadn't heard of Jude's misfortune in the news, he wasn't surprised. Rebels replenished their ranks with pups, training them to hate their very nature if they were half-breeds. Full-blood pups were treated much better and often remained with the rebels after becoming adults.

"Four years," Jude said and returned his gaze to the floor. Another rule taught by the rebels.

Quinn walked over and placed his hand on the pup's shoulder. Jude looked up, meeting his gaze. "I'm sorry for your loss." He held the pup's gaze until Jude nodded. Quinton placed his hand on Alden's shoulder, and met his gaze as well.

"Both of you are safe and welcome here. We've kept this ranch as a safe house for run-away half-breeds for decades and will fight to the death to protect you. As I told you when you arrived, Uncle Ramos and his mate Antwan aren't here at the moment, they took a small group to Canada and will return in a couple days to welcome you properly. In the meantime, if you need anything, just ask."

He smiled at the wave of relief wafting from the two boys who had been at the ranch for three days.

"Thanks, Quinn," Alden gave him his first genuine smile. "I'll get better with training, I promise." His smile slipped and his gaze took on a haunted gleam. "I have to."

"Me, too," Jude said stepping closer to his friend Alden. The two had escaped together and survived. Few pups their age accomplished that feat.

"Let's grab a bite to eat; we'll do this again later." Quinn moved toward the barn, turned into a training area, door. Outside they walked across the yard to the main house and entered. "Go wash up," he told them as he completed a security scan of their property.

A few times over the years, rebels sniffed around their wired acreage, most knew his uncle and his uncle's mate who was a full-blood, and gave the two men a wide berth. But every now and then, a new hot-head tested them. Quinn believed it prudent to always be prepared. He made sure the security system was engaged, pulled the left-over chicken from last night and prepared lunch.

Lunch done, the boys cleaned the kitchen in silence. Quinn sensed they were relaxing their guards, beginning to hope and trust again. Alden hadn't shared his story yet, which wasn't unusual with run-aways. He just hoped the boy would give them a chance to help turn his life around. He contacted his uncle through their mental link. "*Uncle Ramos, how was the placements?*"

Good, all five are settled, finding jobs and becoming acclimated. How are the new boys doing?"

Quinn shared what they'd done today and waited for additional instructions.

"*Sounds good. Antwan and I return tomorrow morning.*"

Glad to hear the two men would arrive sooner than expected, Quinn said. *Perfect timing, I need to pick up a few things from town, including food and that replacement for the broken gate lock came in. Rather than take the pups with me, I'll wait until after you get here."*

His uncle agreed and they disconnected. Quinn took a seat in the oversized stuffed, leather seat in the living room and picked up the remote. Instead of telling the boys what to do, other than a few chores like cleaning the kitchen, he left them alone. A space movie flicked on. Quinn suppressed a groan, and had moved his thumb in position to change the channel when he heard an excited "yes" from behind him. He placed the remote on the arm rest.

Gazes glued to the large flat screen device, Jude and Alden ran toward the long sofa, and plopped down. "I haven't seen anything like this in a couple years," Alden said.

Quinn wanted to ask where, and with who but maintained his silence. His uncle was a master at getting information from those who sought refuge at the ranch and would get the entire story from the pup. If the two weren't who they claimed, his uncle and Antwan would handle them swiftly. The last thing they wanted was drawing Gilbert, Tennessee's Alpha, attention for harboring rebels or breaking the Nation's laws. He yawned and settled more comfortably in the chair. Men on a space station, he snorted as his eyelids drooped.

"Quinn, wake up." Jude shoved him. "You're sitting on the remote."

Without opening his eyes, Quinn fished between the cushion and the chair, pulled out the device and extended it.

"Thanks." And then. "You're snoring. Loud," Alden said.

Jude made a pig-snorkeling sound before bursting into laughter. Alden joined in and soon both made noises they claimed sounded like Quinn.

Amused by their creativity, he smiled but kept his eyes closed. He certainly didn't come across as a wheezing horse, he stretched in the chair and glanced at the credits rolling on the TV. "It's over?"

Smiling, Jude nodded and pointed the remote toward the TV.

"Good," Quinn closed his eyes and wondered if he'd get more sleep. He doubted it but wanted to relax a few minutes longer. In a few hours, they would return to the barn to learn a few basic moves that most pups learned in the nursery.

"My sire snored like that," Alden said.

Quinn stilled.

"Mine too," Jude said. "Not that loud, though."

"Daddy was louder, Mama would tell him to sleep in the living room which was near our bedroom. Many nights I crawled out the window and slept in the tree house."

"Tree house?" Jude said with awe. "You made it?"

"Not by myself. My sire and brothers helped. It was a good place to play and hide." His voice changed on the last word.

Quinn prepared to get involved in the conversation if Alden needed him.

"Sounds like a lot of fun, wish I had one. Weren't no big trees near our house, though. Flat land, easy to see for a long way off," Jude said.

"We had hills, lots of trees, neighbors, a nice house," Alden said in a low voice. Quinn wondered if the pup had shared this information with Jude before.

"Next door neighbors?" Jude asked.

"Close enough to see them, makes them neighbors I think," Alden said.

"At least you had someone to play with," Jude said, with some heat.

"Had three brothers to play with, not neighbors," Alden said. "Alonzo, Alfred, and Albert."

In the background, the Ninja Turtles ruled the airwaves. Quinn assumed the conversation done and mulled over what he learned about Alden.

"Don't know where they are or what happened to them." Alden paused. "We were playing in the backyard, when they came. Mama inside, Sire at work. It was going dark, just before supper. Mam yelled run and I took off, kept going thinking my brothers were behind me. Slammed into a rebel and can't remember anything else from that night."

Alden's tearful words tore at Quinn's heart. Why hadn't La Patron or Alpha Gilbert stopped these atrocities? No pup should be snatched from their den for any reason.

"Hey, you did what your mam said," Jude spoke into the silence. "You did right."

Alden snorted. "She didn't mean run to them, Jude."

"No, but you were what? Four? Five, at the time?" Jude said with conviction that his point was right.

"One day, I'm going to find Taurus and his gang and kill them," Alden said sounding much older than his age. "They stole my life and I plan to take theirs."

"We gotta get stronger and learn how to fight to do that," Jude said.

"You'll help me?" Alden sounded surprised.

"Course. You got me away from them, saved my life. Plus, we're friends," Jude said.

"I'll help you find your sister if you want," Alden said.

"Rosie? She's dead."

Quinn flinched at the flatness in Jude's voice.

"You never said," Alden said in a low tone. "I thought they sent her with the other bitches to breed."

"You gonna look for your brothers?" Jude asked.

"Yes. After."

"If you find your brothers first, you guys could be like ninja turtles and go after the one who stole you. That would be epic," Jude said sounding more like a 10 year-old again.

"It would," Alden said.

"Ask Quinn to take you back home, ask questions, the neighbors may know something." Jude snapped his fingers. "What if your brothers ran to the neighbor's house?"

"Probably did, instead of being dumb like me and going to the woods." A few moments later he continued. "I never dreamed they escaped. What if they did? What if we hadn't been separated and sent to different places like Taurus said?"

Quinn heard the hope and excitement in Alden's voice. It would be a blessing from the Goddess if Alden could be returned to this family. Lack of information prevented Quinn from doing an online search for the boys' families. Now that he knew the particulars for Jude and Alden he would do that tonight.

Tomorrow his uncle would have the information to assist in going forward. If Alden's family lived, nothing would please Quinn more than returning the pup to his sire and mam.

"That would be epic," Jude said with less excitement than before.

"I'll ask Quinn to take me, we can look for them," Alden said, caught up in the possibilities.

"He said if we need anything to ask, want me to wake him?" The ever-helpful Jude asked.

"Yeah. No. Wait. I need to think."

"What's the matter?" Jude asked a few moments later.

"Trying to remember where I lived," Alden said.

"Oh. Tennessee?" Jude asked.

"No, I don't think so," Alden said. "I remember the house with snow. Three other houses on the street," he said.

"Ask Quinn to help," Jude said.

"Not yet. He can't help 'til I remember more," Alden said.

"Oh." Jude sounded disappointed.

Quinn lay in that position until the turtles gave their last hurrah and the boys turned off the TV. He stretched, glanced at them heading down the hall toward their room and mentally promised to teach them everything they needed to know to cut down the bastard who stole their youth.

CHAPTER THREE

Driving was one of Jackie's favorite activities. When she arrived in Dallas nine months ago, she took the test to receive her license. After saving a large portion of her salary for a few months and taking money from her savings, she paid cash for her Mercedes. Buying it herself made the drive more special. She glanced at the dashboard clock, two hours before the dinner meeting with Jonas. That'd give her enough time to shower, change into a pair of comfortable jeans and talk to her mom.

One concession she had to make, her mom backed her dad on this, her home had to be on pack lands. Alpha Theron would have given her a home but she wanted her own space and purchased a three bedroom, three bath, home as far from the Alpha's house as possible. She pulled into the two-car garage and parked.

Twenty minutes later, dressed in a pair of her favorite jeans, tank and slippers, she sunk into the corner chair in her room. She dialed her mom's phone and placed her feet on the large, comfy ottoman.

"Jackie, it's good to hear your voice," her mom said. "I miss you. How's everything going?"

Just hearing her mom's voice filled her with warmth. "I miss you and Daddy too." After asking about her siblings, and their families, she mentioned what happened at work. "Mr. Bradley mentioned me in the department head meeting which I found out later wasn't that good of a thing." Although her mom was more flexible than her dad, she wouldn't appreciate the games Bradley and his team pulled. Slow to anger, but when her mom was angry everyone, except her dad, stayed far away until she calmed down.

"So, proud of you, honey."

"Thanks. Other than that, nothing much has changed since we talked last."

"Are you making friends? I know you and Renee talk every day, but it might be nice to have friends in Houston to hang out with sometimes. Go to a concert or dinner, stuff like that."

That had been Jackie's goal when she moved here but it went south fast. "Not yet. When I first got here I went that route but it became too much work to keep up with their interests."

"Interests?"

"Shopping. Guys. Money. Guys with money to take them shopping." She smiled at her mom' laughter. "I've never been into that stuff. It gives me headaches when Renee wants to hit every store in the mall but I'll do it for her. Nobody else, though. Never understood why any sane person would go to a place just to look in windows." She shivered in disgust.

"Can't you meet people you have more in common with? Join a meet-up group or something to help make life more interesting?"

Jackie hadn't thought of that. Several people in the office joined those groups and did all kinds of things. "That's a good idea, I'll look into it." She paused. "Oh, I'm having dinner with a guy named Jonas." She explained what happened at lunch.

"Sounds interesting."

The way her mom said those two words rang bells. No doubt her father would have a file on the guy before they met for dinner, if he met her dad's approval, she added. "Tango's running a background check and will be with us tonight at dinner. Probably a few more outside."

"Any idea what he wants?" Her mom's lack of comment on the security arrangements meant Alpha Theron had already alerted her parents about the meeting. What if she met a guy she'd like to date? Living outside the compound came at a cost, privacy.

"Not really. He didn't give off vibes like he wanted me to petition you or Daddy for something."

"But you think he wants something?"

Jackie thought about it. "Probably." Breaking the sober turn in the conversation, she said. "What if he's my mate? No one knows when the mating knowledge kicks in. He could be older than Daddy, and already knows I'm his one and only." She placed her fingers over her mouth to keep from laughing.

"What if he is? Will we be planning a wedding soon?"

Jackie frowned. "No. He's too old."

"Like your father? Angus?"

"That's different, he's Daddy and you're you. Age didn't matter back then."

"Back then? In the Stone Ages you mean?"

Jackie laughed. Her mom kept her on her toes and she loved it. "Not quite that old but in the days before electricity, old."

Her mom laughed. "That is old. Although I'm pretty sure we had a television and cell phones growing up."

"I'd like a younger man."

"Younger? A hundred? Two? Is it just 300 that's too old?"

Smiling she sank deeper into her chair. "I want someone who likes the same music I do, with similar experiences and who loves pups."

"This Jonas may have all of those qualities, it's hard to judge a person's age by looking at them." Her mom cleverly boxed her in.

Jackie sighed. "He's not my mate. There was nothing, not a flicker of attraction."

"Ah, I see."

"Where did Nionis go?" She asked to change the conversation.

"A town south of Knoxville, Tennessee. She's teaching at a junior college. Lilly says she likes it there and has hopes of finishing her doctorate soon. Cameron bought her a nice house. Lilly is planning to go visit her in a few months when the kids are out of school."

"Knoxville, that's a strange choice, wonder why she went there?"

"I don't know, according to Lilly she made the decision in one day. She applied for the job, searched Alpha Gilbert's vacant homes and moved within two-weeks. Brendell planned to go with her but changed her mind the night before. Lilly's having a hard time with her now."

"Nionis and Bren were the closest of the older ones," Jackie said thinking of the sweet young girl who had grown into a beautiful young lady. When they were younger, Nionis told Jackie, Brendell had several operations as a young child on her arms and legs. The botched surgeries messed up her limbs, leaving her with an awkward gait and nervous condition that worsened whenever Brendell was upset. When they had sleepovers, Jackie and Nionis would allow Brendell to sleep near them because of her nightmares.

Jackie hoped Nionis' departure hadn't set Brendell back.

"That's part of the problem. Brendell's too afraid to leave the Alpha house, and Nionis has too much energy, drive, ambition, to stay. They're hoping the visit to Nionis in a few months will help Brendell realize she can live in the world without nightmares. If not, Lilly's prepared to allow Brendell to stay as long as she wants."

Jackie thought of her friend and decided to give her a call tomorrow, maybe she could visit during the four-day weekend coming up. "Knoxville's not that far, I might go see Nionis or have her come here. It'd be good hanging with her again," Jackie said, liking the idea more and more. She and Nionis were similar in a no-frills kind of way. Both were straight shooters and preferred not living in gray areas. Even with her gift of sight, Nionis was one of the most level headed people Jackie knew.

"I'm sure she would love that. Make sure you let Tango know, so arrangements can be made," her mom said.

Jackie didn't bother reminding her mom of her top ratings in marksmanship, or hand-to-hand combat, or her ability to pull energy and skills from her three siblings at any time. Jasmine Knight knew all of that and it didn't matter.

"Yes, Ma'am. I'll call Nionis tomorrow, see what's up. I'll let you know what we come up with."

"Sounds, good."

"When's Adam leaving? I'd like to see him before he goes halfway around the world."

"I'm not sure of the exact date, he's still going over paperwork. I think Tomas is more excited about the trip than Adam who seems to be dragging his feet. Oh, Rose is pregnant again."

Thinking of her older brother, Tyrone's mate and one of her favorite people, Jackie jumped up and pumped her fist. "Yes. Yes. Tell her girls this time. Not that I don't love Ryan and Ryder... we need more nieces."

"You have three from Dani and Rese."

"But they had a boy as well, so it cancels it out. Plus, Uncle Angus had two boys, Damian had two boys and one girl, and Asia had two boys. Come on, we need more girls."

"You have a point, call Rose and put in your request. Tell her to have three girls and a boy like Mama and Lilly. That should help balance things."

"I'll tell her when I call her. The compound is over-run with testosterone, just like the military base. I hated staying in the barracks. It always smelled like socks no matter how much I dialed down my senses." She dropped back into her chair and glanced at the clock. "I need to get moving for dinner." She enjoyed talking with her mother because she could share anything with her.

"Alright, let me know how it goes."

"Yes, Ma'am. I want your opinion on it. Love you."

"Love you, too. Be careful."

Jackie picked up her purse, changed shoes in her mudroom, grabbed her jean jacket and went through the garage.

Fifteen minutes later Jackie strode through the door of another steak house with an outstanding national reputation. Tango had been outside her home when she pulled out the driveway and entered the restaurant first. Jonas stood when he saw her and waited at the table until the hostess pulled out her chair before retaking his seat.

With his dark hair combed back, dressed in a black suit, and white collarless shirt, he looked like a pirate from one of the books she'd read.

"Thank you for coming, I appreciate it," he said watching her.

Jackie ordered a sweet tea and lemonade combination, and a plate of calamari.

"Is that all you care to eat?" Jonas asked leaning back in his seat.

"I'm not sure. What did you want to talk about?" No need in wasting time.

He leaned back as the waiter placed a glass of water and her drink in front of her while he sipped what smelled like beer.

When they were alone he tapped, the white linen draped table with his fingertip. A few moments later he leaned forward with his hands clasped together. "My sire owns a fairly decent sized business," he started, surprising her. "Recently he was approached by... a human company to consider selling his business. An offer was made, and accepted. Now we have learned the head of the company has rejected our proposal without explanation."

She held his gaze until the waiter delivered her calamari. Hungry, she picked up a few and popped them into her mouth. "Good," she told the waiter who remained at the side of the table. "I'd like the Chateaubriand, extra sauce on the side with the fresh vegetables and another drink, thank you."

He looked at Jonas. "Would you care for anything, Sir?"

Jonas looked at her. "Will I be joining you for dinner?"

"Probably not," she said as she ate more calamari.

His face didn't change but she sensed his disappointment. When the waiter walked off, she patted her mouth with the napkin. "I don't know why you're telling me this."

Their gazes locked for a few seconds and he leaned back. "I was told you worked for the company and the CEO holds you in high esteem. Earlier today, I picked up a whiff of his scent, which meant you were in close contact with him at some point."

Anger raced through her at his presumption. "Because I sat in a meeting with the CEO, you sought me out to...." She left the sentence hanging. When he didn't say anything, she shook her head at his audacity. "What did all that mean to you?"

"I hoped you would speak to him on our behalf," he said smoothly as if she should've figured it out.

"Why would you hope that? Until this morning I've never seen or heard of you."

"We're pack."

"Then talk to Alpha Theron, your Alpha."

"He's not my Alpha. I'm from Pennsylvania."

"Alpha Samuel, then. Have them intercede on your behalf, not me. I can't do that."

"Can't?"

Now he pushed her buttons. "Won't. I won't go and ask a human CEO about your project just because you're pack. Pack matters go through Alphas. You know that."

"This isn't a pack matter. The company is human-owned."

"Then deal with the company on a human level instead of bringing pack into it," she said, praying for patience.

He nodded, pushed from the table and stood. "I'll leave you to your dinner." He buttoned his coat, offered a stiff bow from the neck down and walked off.

It took everything in Jackie not to watch him walk away, the full-blood gave her the creeps. When her food arrived, she forgot about Jonas and enjoyed her meal.

CHAPTER FOUR

Nionis stood in the airport, just beyond security waiting for Jackie. Excited to see her friend and, in her opinion, the most real of La Patron's den, she moved to get a better view of the deplaning passengers. The wild mass of black curly hair, stood out above the rest of the much shorter people headed for the exit.

Nionis smiled.

Jackie's sun-kissed face, a few shades lighter than Nionis' peanut-butter complexion, glowed as she strode through the crowd. Jackie would be the first to say she wasn't glamorous or beautiful like her twin Renee, but she was wrong. Not that Renee wasn't glamorous; the pup was born that way. Jackie had an earthier beauty, and if she paid the slightest bit attention to the men stumbling and gawking at her long-limbed stride in her snug, fitted, jeans, tee-shirt and ankle boots she would realize it. Fortunately for the males populating the airport, Jackie wore sunglasses, otherwise they'd salivate over her unusual bluish-green eyes. A gift from her sire, La Patron.

Jackie waved and headed toward her.

"I'm so glad you could come," Nionis said as they embraced.

"Me too, I needed to get away without running home. So happy to be in Knoxville. Wahoo hoo!" Jackie raised one arm and pulled her carry-on luggage behind her.

30

Nionis smiled at her friends' antics. "Hungry?"

"Kind of. But I want to do some sight-seeing while I'm here." When they reached the exit, she paused, looked around and waved.

"Who's that?" Nionis asked looking at the full-blood standing across the street.

"Tango, security."

Nionis pointed to a tall, muscular full-blood walking toward them. "This is Chip, security. Chip this is Jackie."

Hi Chip," Jackie said.

He dipped his head and took the luggage. "The car is this way." He turned and walked to the left. Nionis and Jackie followed in silence. Nionis glanced over her shoulder, Tango had disappeared.

An hour later they pulled into the driveway of Nionis home. Considering her uncertain beginning, living in the laboratories of the Liege and then left to die, she thanked the Goddess for her parents' love and generosity. She and her siblings would be dead if it weren't for Lilly and Cameron Knight. Although she lived on pack lands, that had been non-negotiable, she loved her new home and the freedom to work and support herself.

"We're here," she told Jackie who had been fascinated with the history of Knoxville, Gatlinburg and the community college where Nionis worked.

"This is beautiful," Jackie said. "I love the brick. This is a lot of house for one person, something you want to tell me?"

Nionis laughed as they waited for Chip to finish his security check of the house. "Only that Daddy wanted a place big enough for them when they visit. He personally negotiated the deal with Alpha." She shrugged. As long as she got to do what she wanted, it was all good.

Chip walked toward them, nodded and walked to his car. Tango strode into the house in front of them. Nionis waited for Jackie's opinion of her limited interior decorating skills. The furniture was functional, solid wood and soothing neutral cushions, easy to clean fabrics, a step above a minimalist design. She'd always disliked clutter and kept things simple to see everything at a glance.

"Beautiful." Jackie walked to a vibrant painting on the wall. "You framed it."

Nionis nodded. "Our team won which was major considering Renee's talent." In middle school, she, Jackie, and two other kids in their class created this abstract picture and entered it into the art contest. Renee won the overall prize, her work was incredible, but they won a category award for this piece.

"She still says the contest was rigged," Jackie said grinning and pulling out her phone. "I'd like a picture of our middle school masterpiece." She glanced at Nionis.

"Help yourself." She caught Tango's eye and winked.

He smiled and headed outside, locking the door behind him. Nionis fished out her electronics scanner and headed toward the back of the house with it in front of her. When it beeped, and picked up speed she found the small device Tango left behind. Cranking up the scanner's strength, she searched for more listening devices and found three before Jackie came looking for her.

"What do you feel like eating?" Jackie asked coming down the hall.

Nionis checked the blocker in her bedroom to make sure it hadn't been tampered with. "Anything except Mexican food, it still doesn't like me as much as I like it."

Jackie laughed.

"I put you in here." She opened the guest room door which was another master suite. The house had three. The other one was on the top floor with four additional bedrooms. That area was reserved for her parents and siblings.

"Thanks," Jackie said looking around and flopping on the bed. "Feels good."

Nionis jumped on the bed beside her.

Jackie shrieked as she rolled to the side. "Still crazy I see." She smiled as she lay on her side. "*Dating anybody?*" Jackie asked through their link.

"*Not really although Tango looks yummy. Do you have to take him back home with you?*"

Nope, he can stay here as long as you'd like. Jackie paused. *You like working with humans?*"

32

Nionis sighed. "*Some times. A lot of them are really petty and small minded. It's the rest with the big hearts and bright spirits that draw you in. I don't spend a lot of time with other staff members.* 'She pointed to her right eye. *I see too much of them to be comfortable. But the kids... most are amazing. I get to draw them out and teach what they need to move forward in life, that's worth it for me.*"

Thanks, I needed to hear that." Jackie shared a little from her job and the challenges she'd recently faced with projects. *Honestly, I don't know where he's getting these projects, most of them have holes large enough for a tank truck to ride through.*"

That's because your brain is wired to see those holes, most aren't." Nionis sat up. "*Why didn't I think of that?*"

What?"

You. You see things too, just differently, 'Nionis said thinking fast. Could Jackie help with her side project? Maybe. But should she open that door? She glanced at Jackie. *I never explained why I came here.*"

Jackie shook her head as she sat up facing Nionis. *No.*"

Some might think what she planned to do was treasonous. She hoped Jackie knew her well enough to listen as her friend and not La Patron's daughter. Nionis cleared her throat. *After I finished my Master's Degree, I toured Europe searching for clues about my family. That was a disaster.* 'She thought about the 11 months of chasing clues, and the life's lessons she had learned and changed her position. *Not a disaster but I didn't discover anything about my past.*"

Jackie placed her arm Nionis' shoulder and pulled her close. *I'm sorry.*"

Nionis inhaled and pushed through those dark memories. *Next came a couple months of blahs. I didn't want to do much, just hung around the house. Mama was worried. Your mom too. But I couldn't get over that zero of a trip, know what I mean?*"

Jackie nodded but didn't say anything.

One night, I woke up. Just sat straight in the bed, alert. Got out of bed and turned on my laptop. This job was the first thing I saw on my thread. 'She read the curiosity in her friend's gaze. "*You ever get the feeling that this is what you should be doing at this moment in time?*"

No, not yet."

It's hard to explain how it grips you and doesn't let go. There's no room for doubt, uncertainty flies out the window and you can't articulate the urgency you feel other than you have to do or be in a certain place."

Jackie nodded. Sounds intense."

It was. I applied for the job right then, didn't wait until morning. Soon I as downloaded all my information I searched the news for the area. I figured had to be more than the job pulling me here. 'She read Jackie's interest and pulled out her phone. Once she had a map on the screen she showed it to her friend. In the past three years, these states, Georgia, Tennessee, and North Carolina, has had sightings of young pups living in the mountains. I tracked articles for the past 10 years so far and there are more."

You think your family's in the mountains?" Jackie asked.

No. I wish but no. My family lives in the Alpha house in West Virginia, that's good enough for me."

Jackie nodded.

Then I saw it."

Your vision?"

Nionis nodded. Indirectly. Rebels attacked this family living on the outskirts of pack lands. Two of the four pups were taken; the mam was hurt but survived. The sire came home from work and went searching for his pups. He found one dead in the mountains, no one knows what happened to the other one."

Rebels come that close to pack lands?" Jackie asked looking at the map.

Not as much anymore but a few years back they went through a wave, hitting areas and taking pups."

Jackie looked at her. Pups?"

Nionis nodded. "Yep. Before their wolves develop to keep them out of the system."

And off the Alpha's radar. 'Jackie stared at the map again.

Nionis hoped Jackie wouldn't tell her siblings everything, not yet anyway.

This is what drew you here? 'Jackie asked meeting Nionis' gaze.

I think so. I've taken a few drives into the mountains south of Gatlinburg off 441 for preliminary searches and there's more of our people up there than in the databases."

Jackie frowned. *There's a reason you haven't told Alpha Gilbert."*

Nionis treaded carefully. *"Yes. I think I'm supposed to do something, maybe help someone. I don't know. But I'm uneasy about reporting what I feel. Until I understand better what's what, I'm keeping quiet.* 'She hoped Jackie would keep quiet as well but couldn't ask that of her.

Chip doesn't see or feel what you feel?"

No. We've been up there three times and he doesn't sense anything. At least that's what I think anyway. He's never said anything."

So, it's metaphysical, through your special vision," Jackie said meeting Nionis gaze.

That's what brought me here, I'm sure of it. 'She nodded.

Then you have to follow through on it. The Goddess gifted you for bigger things than helping us win against the guys in finders-seekers. 'Jackie smiled.

Nionis laughed at the reference to the game they played as pups. *Hey, that was fun until they caught on what we were doing."*

Only because your brother called David and told him you were helping us from the Alpha house. Mama said it wasn't fair because the boys didn't have help, 'Jackie said.

My brothers were such tattlers back then, now you can't get anything out of them. Pierre's moving but won't tell me squat. 'She shook her head, relieved to have shared what was fast becoming a burden.

Before I leave I want to ride with you to the mountains. Look the place over. A helicopter might be better, I may see something that will help, 'Jackie said, surprising Nionis. *Also, I want to see Gatlinburg."*

That's awesome; I'll have Chip set it up. 'She jumped up, held out her hand. *Enough of that, let's go eat."*

Jackie stood. Together they left for dinner.

CHAPTER FIVE

Quinn heard the hum of the helicopter overhead as he headed into town on Highway 441. Ramos and Antwan arrived before sunrise, and would work with the pups today. Last night, Quinn researched Alden's story and discovered the pup's family had moved but were alive. He contacted the pup's sire whose joy brought them both to tears. It was rare to reconnect stolen pups to their families. Alden's sire would fly in for him today. He offered to take Jude as well which would be great for the young pup. Ramos and Antwan agreed and would handle the details.

Packages and groceries loaded in the SUV, Quinn headed for a coffee shop off Main street. They had a special roasted blend he enjoyed and a sexy, red headed half-breed he enjoyed more. Entering the shop, Paula, the half-breed he hooked up with on occasion smiled at him.

He winked, looked at his watch and then back at her. Her smile widened. He would wait in town until she went to lunch and go back to her place with her. Glad to have that arrangement taken care of he placed his order and walked outside to clear his nose.

"Excuse me."

Quinn took a sip from his cup and eyed the delicious dish walking toward him. Smooth peanut-butter skin, large hazel-gray eyes and a head full of dark, short curls. Not bad. If he hadn't made arrangements with Paula... he stiffened. She wasn't human. His wolf was submerged, and undetectable, or he should be. "Yes?"

"I'm Nionis. I just moved to the area, can I talk to you for few minutes?"

Quinn frowned. "Why?"

Her right eye brightened or flashed, he wasn't sure which but it was disconcerting. "Because you can help me. I've been running in circles and here you are."

"What?" The woman made no sense.

She leaned forward. "Missing pups."

Everything inside him froze. "What are you talking about?"

She wore an exasperated expression, looked over her shoulder and back at him. "I have this... this gift." She waved to her face. "It's led me to this area, then I saw you and I knew you were involved. I just... it's frustrating to come against so many roadblocks. But I know I'm supposed to do something to help." She shook her head.

Her passionate response resonated true, no doubt she was sincere. But there were too many lives on the line to talk no matter what.

"Miss, I have no idea what you're talking about." He moved the right, scenting the area. There were full-blood strangers nearby. That wasn't a surprise, but her approaching him, coupled with full-bloods didn't bode well.

She placed her hand on his arm, gave him her business card. "Please take this. Contact me when the need arises. I will help." When he didn't take the card, she stuck it in his pocket.

"Lady, you're crazy." He backed up, with his one free hand in the air in case anyone watched.

"Yeah, you pegged me." She smiled and he appreciated her not following him.

Quinn walked down the street without looking back. Crossing the street, he headed into an arcade. Inside, a few half-breeds assisted customers and paid him little attention. Pleased they hadn't recognized his wolf, he released a breath.

Gazing out the window, he searched for Nionis. She and another female walked into the restaurant next to the coffee shop.

Nionis was very pretty, but the black-haired siren with her was nothing short of perfection. A few shades lighter and taller than Nionis, with curves that made his beast howl in appreciation. He wondered if she was a tourist passing through Gatlinburg or visiting Nionis.

Coffee finished, he played with the idea of lunch in the restaurant. He glanced at his watch. Too much time before Paula's lunch break. He played a few games but his concentration was shot to hell. Irritated, he headed to the restaurant. Immediately, he scented the strange full-bloods that sat at a table near the front and looked at him when he entered.

Quinn took the menu the waitress offered. He relaxed when the full-bloods ignored him and continued their meal. He placed a to-go order and waited at the end of the bar. It didn't take long for Nionis to approach him.

"Hey, you never told me your name," she said coming to stand next to him.

"No, I didn't." He glanced toward the full-bloods who watched them for a few seconds.

"I'm Nionis, this is my friend Jackie," she said.

He looked at the woman he'd seen earlier and promptly forgot to breathe.

"Hello," she said. Her smile faltered as the silence lengthened.

"Speak asshole," Nionis muttered as she kicked his shin.

"Ow." He glared at her and then looked at the other one who scattered his thoughts. "Hello."

The two full-bloods stood. One headed toward them, the other toward the door. Great, 30 years of undetected living off the grid and gone in less than an hour.

"Let's go," Jackie said to Nionis, glancing at him as if he lacked wits or something.

That bothered him. "I'm Quinn," he said without thinking why that was a horrible idea.

Nionis smile brightened. "Do you live around here? My friend's visiting from Dallas, and we're sight-seeing. Any suggestions on what we should see?"

He read the question in her eyes, the need to know more. "Not really, everything's good, the arcade, the amusement park, hiking." He shrugged, keeping the big full-blood who sat at the front of the bar in his peripheral vision.

"Hiking sounds like fun," Nionis said, eyes lit with mischief.

Quinn glanced at Jackie. "What color are your eyes? I don't think I've ever seen that color?" he asked before his brain connected to his mouth. What the hell was he doing? He never talked to humans like this.

She chuckled, a cute sound that hit him in his gut, twisted him in knots and refused to let him go. This wasn't good.

"Blue and green. They change based on circumstances." She pulled a few strands of hair behind her ear and looked over his shoulder. "We've walked around the amusement park already, any suggestions which is the best trail for hiking?"

He spewed off a few that were in all the brochures away from the ranch.

"Thanks," she said as he retrieved his to-go items and paid his bill.

"Want to join us?" Nionis asked, her tone daring him to say no.

Paula walked in, saw him and waved. "Sorry, I can't. I have a prior engagement."

One of the full-bloods stood in front of Paula and then looked over his shoulder at Quinn with murder in his eyes. Quinn held the man's gaze for a few seconds and then looked at Paula who stared at the full-blood with her mouth opened and eyes wide. She threw her arms around the giant and they walked out without a backward glance.

"What the hell just happened?" he whispered. "That was my date." He took a few steps in Paula's direction.

"Whoa, buddy." Nionis grabbed his arm. "Don't do it. Whatever she was to you is in the past, Tango will rip you apart if you go near her again."

Frowning, he stared at her. "Why? We've known each other for years."

Nionis leaned close to his ear. "That's his wife, mate. They've been looking for each other for years and just found each other."

"Wife?" The word mate screamed at him. The rest of her explanation was for any of his kind listening and thinking him human. Still, he couldn't believe Paula's luck. She was a nice person and he wished her the best.

Nionis nodded, watching him closely.

"Didn't know she was married. Thanks for letting me know." He nodded at Nionis and met Jackie's calm gaze. "Nice meeting you, enjoy your visit." *Would you be willing to take Paula's place?* he thought, hoping his boner would soften so he could walk without discomfort. Quinn nodded to the women and walked off.

Outside, he cleared his nostrils but couldn't shake the pleasure he'd felt standing next to Jackie. It was electric. He scoffed at the poetic nature of his words as he headed toward the parking area to his truck.

"Quinn," Paula called from the other side of the street standing next to her glaring mate.

"Be happy." He waved, glad to see the smile light her face as she snuggled closer to the wolf. When he reached his vehicle, he hesitated. *Jackie.* He rolled her name on his tongue and smiled at the delightful tingles. She was the first human to ever hold his attention. Not that he'd do more than think about her. Humans didn't interest him, at least until now.

Jackie watched the human swagger out the restaurant with mixed feelings. That she had feelings at all surprised her.

"What did you think?" Nionis asked.

About you throwing us at him?" Jackie asked as they turned to leave. Chip led and another security person took up the rear.

Kind of reminds you of David, doesn't he?"

Jackie jerked. *My brother David?"*

Nionis nodded.

Not at all. David wouldn't have given you his name or talked to you." Her brother wasn't stuck up but he wasn't friendly either. You had to warm up to him or he had to warm up to you, before you saw the person his siblings and close friends saw.

Exactly how he acted until you showed up. That's why I called you over." She bumped Jackie with her hips. *You got skills, loosened his tongue. Poor thing probably didn't realize he said what he did."*

Secretly pleased, Jackie shook her head. *"Wasn't me who got him talking, girl. That was all you. Wanna bet he had plans with Tango's mate?"*

Nope, you'd win. Bet you'll have a new security person here before we leave Gatlinburg. No way his mate will stomach him being around a single bitch.' She winked at Jackie.

That's not a bet, it's a statement of fact.' She waved at Tango. He walked over to them.

"Ladies this is Paula Bronson, my mate. Paula this is Jackie." He pointed to her, it was decided to forgo last names and not broadcast her connection to La Patron. He pointed to Nionis and introduced her.

"Hi Paula."

"Hello," the preppy looking blonde said with her hands wrapped around Tango's arm.

"Tango I'm so happy for you. Alpha Theron is going to be happy," Jackie said and meaning it. Although wolves could have long relationships and pups with either half-bloods, full-bloods or human breeders, having a mate-bond was the gold ring.

He nodded and kissed Paula's temple. "Earlier I thought I sensed her ... but I wasn't sure and couldn't go look. But the Goddess smiled on me and sent this little one to me."

"Not to you," Jackie thought keeping her smile in place.

"Chip, we want another helicopter ride," Nionis said. Chip nodded and left.

"Going back in the air?" Tango asked concerned.

Nionis shrugged. "We're not going to hike, might as well see all we can." She faced Paula. "Does Quinn live in the mountains?"

Nionis," Jackie snapped, even though she was interested in Paula's response.

Tango stiffened and then eased up a bit.

"I thought he lived in Knoxville or somewhere like that," Paula said. "I only see him when he comes to town."

"Why Knoxville?" Nionis asked.

Jackie wanted to know as well.

Paula shrugged. "Just the way he speaks, his manners, real polite, smart, quirky sense of humor. He won't start trouble but if trouble finds him, he'll finish it. He's got that kind of vibe." She rubbed Tango's arm. "But not as much as Tango."

Jackie stopped her eye roll at Paula's attempt to ease Tango's wolf. Newly mated, Paula would learn how to handle Tango, few men, especially wolves were okay with their mates admiring anyone else. Her dad made that clear to their mom on a few occasions.

"Let's go," Jackie told Nionis as she turned in the direction of the copter rentals leaving her friend behind. Out the corner of her eye she saw a small, grimy faced girl peek at her from the side of a building. Curious, she waved.

The child ducked and disappeared. Jackie walked to the edge of the single-story building, looked down the length of the wall but it was empty.

I'm ready, 'Nionis said walking up to her. *What're you looking at?*" She looked at the side of the building.

A little girl, at least I think it was a girl was hiding and watching us, 'Jackie said through their link to keep Tango and Chip from hearing them.

Nionis walked to the side of the building and ran around back. Jackie pulled out her phone, took a few pictures of the building for reference. Nionis hadn't reappeared. Chip would return for them any minute. Pretending to read text messages, Jackie tapped her feet wishing she could join her friend but knew it would draw more attention to the child and Nionis' mission.

Nionis cleared the building with a satisfied gleam. *Saw her. There are two of them, half-bloods. Someone whisked them away before I could reach them.* 'Nionis looked over her shoulder, Chip waved them forward. *Good, maybe we can see them from the air.*" She jogged in the direction of the helicopter rentals building.

Jackie followed at a brisk pace with conflicting emotions. "*What's wrong?*" her brother David asked.

I'm not sure. We're going for a helicopter ride over the mountains."

You've done that before."

Jackie wasn't ready to share her friend's secret and made sure that part of her thoughts was locked down tight. "*Still makes me uneasy.*"

David chuckled and it was good to hear. "*If you need me, I'm here to hold your hand.*"

She stepped into the copter, strapped in and took the offered headset. "*Thanks, will do.*"

Nionis stared out the window as the full-blood pilot gained altitude. She gave him directions and pulled out a pair of binoculars.

Where did you get those? 'she asked pointing.

The pilot, 'Nionis said looking down.

Each vehicle heading away from town, Jackie wondered if it was Quinn. Where did he go so fast? To find another woman? Possibly.

How old do you think that guy was? 'she asked Nionis.

"*What guy? Quinn?*"

Jackie nodded.

Seemed young, older than us but not by much."

Jackie agreed.

He liked you. Most men do, but the way his eyes lit when he looked at you helped a lot, 'Nionis said.

Strange that I'm thinking about him, don't you think. It's not unusual to think about humans, but... he looked good, 'Jackie said.

For a few moments Nionis didn't respond. Jackie looked at her. *You see something?*"

Maybe, but it's not there now."

Could be warded? 'Jackie said thinking of what Sarita told them about her Nana's pack lands.

What? 'Nionis frowned.

Jackie told her Amynta, Sarita's grandmother used some type of incantation to ward her land to keep people from seeing and entering it.

Nionis stared at her and then pulled out her phone.

What're you doing? 'Jackie asked when Nionis opened an app.

Getting the coordinates of the area. I'll have him fly back over."
A few moments later the copter turned and Nionis tapped a few keys on her phone. She nodded with satisfaction. *Is there anywhere else you want him to take us?* 'She looked at Jackie.

Unsure what that look in her friend's eye meant, Jackie shook her head. "*What's going on? What do you plan to do with those coordinates?*"

Going hunting."

Puzzled by the excitement leaping in her chest by the two words, Jackie leaned back against the cushions with one certainty. She wouldn't be returning to Houston in two days.

CHAPTER SIX

Quinn's thoughts remained in town on the black-haired beauty with the aquamarine eyes. She hadn't said much, but he'd bet she saw everything. He still couldn't believe he had blurted his name like that. There were beautiful women in the pack, so it wasn't just her pretty face. For some reason, she snagged his beast's attention. Considering how deep he'd locked the animal side of his nature down, that shouldn't have happened.

He frowned.

Was she a threat? Was his beast issuing a warning? In the safety of his vehicle, Quinn released the rein, his beast surfaced, sniffing the air. As he reached a bend in the road, a familiar van pulled onto the highway behind him. Inhaling, he recognized the scent of one of his uncle's scouts. After all this time, the full-bloods refused to give names and wore masks as if Quinn couldn't identify them by scent. Per protocols, he would continue to the ranch but stop at a copse of trees in another mile to make the exchange. Quinn contacted his uncle, and got his approval to make the pick-up.

When the exchange point came into view, Quinn pulled off the road and drove a short distance down the rocky incline until he couldn't be seen from above or the road. The van pulled behind him a few moments later. Tense, Quinn waited for the scout to exit the van. Inhaling, he verified the scent and watched a small girl and slightly taller one exit the door.

Female runaways were rare. Rebels and rival full-bloods kept them on lock-down for breeding. Moving slowly, they headed for his SUV. Once they reached the doors he stepped out, nodded to the scout who had returned behind the wheel of the van. Receipt acknowledged, the van backed up as Quinn opened the door.

"Hello, my name is Quinn. I'll take you to a place of safety." The smallest child shrank against the larger and he wondered if they were siblings. Once inside, he admonished them to fasten their seat-belts as he locked the door.

The whoomph of helicopter engines flew overhead. Quinn eased into his seat, buckled up and looked in the rear-view mirror. "We'll wait a few minutes until that copter heads back to town."

The taller girl nodded and lowered her head.

"I've got bottled water in the back if you're thirsty." He pointed to the bottles on the passenger seat floorboard.

"Yes, two please," the older girl said in a strained voice.

Glad for some communication, he leaned forward, grabbed the plastic bottles and handed them to her. The sound of the copter had waned, now it came back strong.

"Are they looking for us?" the older girl asked after taking several gulps of water.

"I don't know, could they be?" What had these girls done?

She shrugged and hunched down in her seat looking up as if she could see through the roof. No one spoke until the sound disappeared. Quinn started the engine, pulled back onto the highway and headed for the ranch. Something happened to these girls, there was too much fear, sorrow and determination in the gaze of the older one.

Five miles before the ranch entrance, they drove through a covered bridge which triggered the ward covering the ranch and verified his identity. If an enemy or trespasser came through the bridge, the road would veer in directions leading them away from the ranch.

Quinn pulled into the barn.

Uncle Ramos waved in greeting from the wide entrance and approached the truck with his hand-held scanner. With one hand, he assisted the older girl out of the vehicle while introducing himself and scanning her. He repeated it with the smaller child. Pleased they weren't wired, internally or externally, he escorted them to the house, leaving Quinn to unload the supplies.

Hours later at dinner, Antwan gave the report on Alden and Jude's good fortune. "Alden's father accepted Jude on the spot, hugged and showed him the ticket he'd purchased for him to go home with them. Should've seen Jude's eyes light up, glad he wouldn't separate from Alden. Turns out those two have been through more than we thought. Alden's sire wept hearing what befell his pup and agreed to help search for Taurus and put an end to him."

"You found his family?" Wide-eyed, Marsha the older teen asked.

"Yes, we try to reconnect families," Ramos said gently.

Through a barrage of tears, the 14-year-old told Ramos of her two miscarriages and the mental and physical abuse she endured since being taken from her family at the age of eight. When she saw, them grooming Penny, the younger girl with her, something inside snapped. She made plans for them to escape or die trying.

"We'll search for your family first," Ramos said as he reached over and covered her hand with his.

She smiled.

Quinn saw the makings of a beautiful woman, despite her horrific beginnings.

"I never dreamed." She shook her head. "They said our families were gone, that they were the only ones we had. But if his father came for him, it's all a lie, isn't it?" She stared at Ramos.

"They lied to steal your hopes and dreams, little one. To call what they put you through a family is an insult. When you are ready, tell us what you remember of home and we will search for both of you."

Marsha's face dropped as she looked at Penny, the smaller one. "Thank you. Penny goes with me."

"Of course," his uncle said.

"Her family's with them. They can never get her. Never," Marsha hissed.

Penny rubbed her arm.

For a few moments, no one spoke. "Is there something you need to tell us?" Antwan asked leaning back in his chair with his arms crossed. Of the five people, sitting at the table, he was the most imposing, at 6'5" and almost 300 pounds of muscle. He dwarfed his mate's 5'11" rounder, stature. They used their differences to their advantage when dealing with people.

Marsha's gaze flew to Antwan and she looked away immediately. Seconds passed as she visibly straightened and met his gaze again. "Her parents are part of the rebels. She was given to Taurus for breeding, but he's out of town. They were holding her until he came back and then... then he'd have her." She inhaled and visible shuddered. "She's just started...she's only nine. It's not her fault her body changed so early. Look at her. She has the mind of a six or seven year-old, no matter what her body does."

Quinn threw his napkin on the table. "Bastards." Penny looked at him. Their gazes connected and she smiled innocently at him through the clear gray eyes.

"Had no idea they were breeding babes," Antwan said rubbing his chin.

"Taurus again," Ramos said glancing at his mate. The two exchanged glances before he spoke to Marsha. "Have you seen him?"

She blinked. "Taurus?"

Ramos nodded and muttered. "It's one name he goes by."

"I think so. When we first come in, he talks to newbies, explains what they do and why. He's convincing at first, gets you to stop being scared. Then we're passed along, to others for training and breeding."

"Could you describe him, height, weight, anything that would help find him?" Antwan asked.

Her gaze flew from Ramos, to Quinn, to Antwan. "Yes. I'll tell you what I remember."

"Will you contact Alden if we go after Taurus?" Quinn asked his uncle.

"I think that's only fair," Ramos said after a few moments. "It'll free his nightmares and help him move forward."

"He's not the only one," Marsha muttered.

"What else do you know?" Ramos asked her.

"When we first came in, Taurus acts like they're some secret pack that's all about full-bloods. But he lives between the human world and ours. I'm surprised he hasn't been caught by now," Marsha said sounding much older than a 14-year-old, which was a shame.

"Human world?" Antwan said. "In what way?"

"I'm not sure. When I lost the pups this last time, I overheard them speaking that he was out of town working some deal with humans. Something to do with money and how they hoped he got it soon, they need more money for supplies," she said.

"That's where you escaped from? The medical facility?" Quinn asked thinking to go after the place and close it down.

"No. But, being there kept me closer to a real town so I could escape. The clinic's in the mountains, they kept us in a house near there."

"Could you tell us how to find it?" Antwan asked picking up the direction of Quinn's thoughts.

Marsha closed her eyes and told them what she remembered.

Antwan nodded. "I think I know the area. A vet had a clinic there for years."

"Explains the animal smells in the place," Marsha said frowning.

Antwan looked at Quinn.

He smiled. "Animal smells?"

"Indeed," Antwan said with a small grin. "Seems like a visit to the doc is in order."

Dressed in all black, feeling more alive than ever, Jackie followed Nionis over the high fence and landed near a decorative statue and concrete bench.

"*What kind of place is this?*" Jackie asked.

"*Veterinary clinic. I've come here before and wanted to check it out. Inhale. There are more than animals in there. I think this may be a place where they smuggle pups.*" She pulled out a circular device, waved it around slowly and pointed to the right. After clicking a few buttons, she waved Jackie along.

No longer surprised by Nionis' "spy" tools, as Jackie called them, she followed her friend while sending a prayer to God and the Goddess for their safety. She refused to think what her father would say about this night-time jaunt into the mountains without security.

There's somebody else here."

What? Where?" Jackie hated being blind but she promised her parents to remain human deep when in public. Sneaking away without security broke one rule, she wasn't going to compound things by breaking more.

Well, I'll be damned. Quinn and another... guy's with him. Wonder what they're doing here? Let's wait, see how things pan out. Seems Quinn knows more than he let on," Nionis said.

Jackie's stomach clenched at his name. All day she'd pushed aside memories of their short encounter. No matter how she replayed the day, she didn't see what Nionis claimed. The man wasn't interested in her.

Let's go back over the wall, look for their car," Jackie said relieved to come up with a plan to keep them from trespassing.

Nionis smiled. *Great idea. It'd be interesting to hear Quinn's explanation and see what they're doing."*

They leapt across the fence and searched for Quinn's scent. A few moments later they found a large, black, SUV parked a couple miles from the vet's clinic. Nionis slipped something beneath the trunk and waved Jackie away from the vehicle. They hid behind nearby trees. It didn't take long for what sounded like a war to break out. Gunshots, yells, screams, a loud boom, the ground shuddered and finally a whooshing sound.

Jackie's gaze widened as fire licked the roof of a corner of the building. "*We need to help."* She pulled Nionis' arm.

Let's wait." She looked at Jackie. *Listen. Those screams weren't four legged and it wasn't that many of them."*

Straining to hear, Jackie loosened the rein on her beast for a second to verify Nionis' words and slammed it back down. Chills ran down her back as she stared into the dark. *They're coming."*

Good. I have a few questions for Quinn," Nionis said.

He's not alone. They have... pups, I think, with them," Jackie said battling her wolf to remain hidden and trying to think through the problem of why it was so hard to do so.

Nionis placed her hand on Jackie's shoulder. *Are you okay?"*

Jackie took a deep breath and slammed the cage on her beast. "*Yeah, for a minute there."* She turned toward the SUV. A man as tall and wide as her father and older brothers approached the small clearing with a child in his arm. Quinn strode behind him holding another child. Two small kids walked between them.

Jackie's chest tightened in gratitude as she watched the gentle manner the giant placed the child in the back of the SUV. She jumped when he turned, reached out and held Nionis arm in his grip. She hadn't seen anyone move that fast since interning with Cain and the Knights at the Pentagon.

"Who are you?" he growled down at Nionis and glanced in Jackie's direction.

"Nionis. Hey, Quinn, need any help?" She called ignoring the giant, as Quinn helped the others into the SUV.

"No." He didn't look in their direction. When the last child settled, he closed the door and slid into the driver's seat.

Without thinking, Jackie ran toward the passenger side, opened the door and slid into the front seat. "We can help."

Quinn did a double take and glared at her. "What? No."

"We're going. You have pups, we can help," Jackie said unsure why she pressed the issue.

He shook his head, looked up and then at her. "There's a fire. Trucks are on the way. We have to go," his voice rose with each word.

She pulled the scat-belt across her waist. "Stop wasting time. Let's go."

The back of the truck opened. Antwan slid inside, Nionis with him. Jackie had no idea what happened between those two, but sirens in the distance stopped all discussions. Quinn started the truck and they took off down the road, avoiding emergency vehicles.

Ignoring the hostility wafting off Quinn, Jackie looked at the two children huddled on the seat behind her. Silent tears rolled down the face of the smallest one. The other stared blankly at the back of Quinn's seat. Jackie unsnapped her seat belt, crawled between the seats and sat between them. The smaller one's tears tugged her heartstrings, she pulled him on her lap, and hugged him tight.

"You smell good," the little one said, snuggling closer. Reaching over, she pulled the silent pup close to her side and hugged him tight.

"Are you the Goddess?" the little one asked and yawned.

"No. But I think she wanted me here with you tonight," she whispered near his ear. So very small, when last had they eaten? Full-bloods or half-breeds? Not that it mattered, they were pack. How had this happened? Alphas were in place in every state to take care of pack, yet these pups were malnourished, cold and abused.

Mama would be so pissed, Jackie thought. Her mom had a network of women across the country, she called them "eyes and ears" of the Nation who prevented strangers from preying on their people. Did they monitor rebel activity? Jackie wasn't sure but planned to check into it.

Any idea where we're going?" Jackie asked Nionis. *"If this is something against the Nation, I can't not report it. You know that, right?"*

Yeah, same here. But this big guy, Antwan, full blood is mated to a breed and he claims they help runaways."

Jackie was surprised. *"He told you that?"*

Actually, I told him they helped runaways, he didn't deny it. He has a guy's name tattooed on his arm."

Like Quinn, Antwan didn't seem like the type to over share information or give strangers a ride. Nionis must've passed some kind of test. *These pups are suffering, it's heartbreaking."*

"This may sound backward, but where will the children go now for health care? At least they had a place, now it's gone," Nionis said.

Jackie hadn't thought of that. *"Something to ask when we arrive wherever we're going."*

I intend to."

So far your intuition has been on point. Are we on the right track?"

Yes, I'm peaceful and hopeful at the same time about this."

Jackie nodded and placed another kiss on the forehead of the small boy in her lap. In the rear-view mirror her gaze met Quinn's. He held hers for a few seconds and then released it.

Can you hold off telling anybody about this until we learn more?" Nionis asked surprising Jackie.

Yeah. If they're able to rescue pups and help them, they're doing something the Alphas and KnightForce haven't been able to do. Pups are more important than politics. 'She hoped that promise wouldn't bite her in the ass.

CHAPTER SEVEN

Taurus slammed his fist on the table in the corner of his office, stood and walked to the window. Everywhere he went, he smelled the foul, stench of half-breeds. They populated like damn rabbits. If full-blood bitches didn't breed more than one litter in their life-time, their beloved nation would be lost to mutts.

The raid at the clinic last night smacked of Ramos and Antwan, or as he thought of them, Beavis and Butthead. Those two butted into matters that didn't concern them often costing him money, time and resources. Something would need to be done about them.

Rather than obsess over the two older men he changed gears. "Where are the parents?" he asked his assistant, Oliver over the monitor.

"At the hotel. They'd just signed all the papers giving the pups to us for training."

Going in for physicals was the next step in the process. If the pups were human, his group could argue in court for their return. But La Patron ruled the legal system for wolves with an iron fist and would destroy them all before returning the pups.

"Did you compensate them for the trip and hotel?" Taurus asked growing weary of bad news. They could not afford to lose more faithful followers. Most of these pups were bred by half-breeds they had taken in raids and won over for their cause. They provided cannon-fodder but little else.

"Yes. They're stocking up on supplies before returning home."

"Good. I'll be in meetings the rest of the day."

"Another thing. Penny, the full-blood gift for you," Oliver said.

Penny, a young full-blood, was taken from Canada specifically for him to breed. He had been so busy raising funds for their cause he'd forgotten about her.

"Has she arrived?" Taurus asked visualizing the petite beauty.

"Yes, but she ran away with another breeder, Marsha. From what I was told, Marsha miscarried again at the clinic. Penny was there being examined. They were in the holding house when they escaped."

Taurus froze. "The clinic that burned down?"

Oliver gasped. "Yes. Within 48 hours of their escape. Do you think the arsonists had inside help?"

Taurus' hand curled into a fist. "I'm thinking Marsha told them about the clinic, that stupid bitch. I'll kill her." In his mind, he choked the useless bitch to death with his bare hands. Not only had she lost two litters but she took something that belonged to him.

"Who did she tell?" Oliver asked.

Taurus wouldn't release the names. He and Ramos had history but the man went too far by destroying the clinic *and* taking Penny.

"Never mind that, I'll handle it. Contact the Locators. I want Penny found, and Marsha alive. It's been a while since I made an example out of someone for betrayal." Using human bounty hunters came in handy when dealing with Ramos and Antwan. Those two shied away from human law-men but would kick a wolf's ass into next week. "Give them just enough information to get them started."

"A modified copy of the contract between you and Penny's parents?" Oliver asked as if that document existed.

Taurus laughed. "Yes, that has a nice touch." Eager to finish the conversation, review the details of the damage and get back to his other meetings before his dinner meeting, he glanced at his watch. "What else?"

"Supplies arrived to the warehouse on time and we're in the process of shipping them to the three villages. Doc wasn't at the clinic, we lost his assistant though. He needs help and can't take the time to properly train anyone right now. His words, not mine. We're going to need a new medical facility."

The responsibilities of a revolution never ended. Patriots were required to give more than their life to the vision of a nation with full-blood rule, himself included.

"Fire up our base, tell them what we need, get a few volunteers to shadow Doc, maybe record what he's doing for future training." He paused thinking of a new clinic location and one stuck in his mind. "I'll get back to you later this week regarding a building. I'm thinking of a large place in the mountains with a basement we can convert. The clinic's basement held supplies and didn't have enough headroom to walk around so everyone was above ground, making them targets. With a basement, we can install blockers to screw-up any scans." He pursed his lips, thinking of the possibilities.

Despite the temporary set-back and loss of a few lives, securing a better clinic would make them all safer in the long term. His contact assured him they would have more than enough money for supplies and to purchase another building. "This may not be so bad, I'll get back with you." He disconnected and sat at his desk.

Ramos. The wily old man had been around longer than dirt, helped hundreds of their people, including Taurus, his mam and sire survive against La Patron's harsh rule for decades.

Antwan, a fierce, warrior from some Indian clan, doted on Ramos and would kill Taurus or anyone who posed a threat to his mate. Too many people watched out for those two, even rebels gave the ranch a wide berth, to mount a direct attack. If he went after them he'd need to pick them off away from the ranch, which seemed more impossible.

Securing a full-blood female had been extremely difficult and costly. He doubted his people could pull it off any time soon. He needed to breed Penny. Hopefully she'd give him a large litter to train. The idea of his own pups excited and motivated him to make breeding her a reality.

Scenario after scenario rolled through his mind, none presented a safe way to retrieve Penny. He closed his eyes against the probable loss. How would they usher in an era of full-blood supremacy without more full-bloods? He pulled up the statistics on his cell. While their numbers were a couple thousand, that was a drop against La Patron's millions. Perhaps he should relocate to another country, he had sent scouts to Canada and Mexico to search for large plots of land.

Leaning back in his chair, he crossed his hands over his flat belly after smoothing his crisp white shirt. "Why do we have to move?" The idea of leaving the land of his birth rankled. Half-breeds were the anomaly, an experiment gone wrong. If full-bloods didn't mate with half-breeds, the rebels would have won long ago.

Tired, Taurus exhaled, and stood without making a decision on what to do about Penny or Ramos. Maybe the Goddess would favor them for a change with a way to retrieve Penny and take out Ramos.

CHAPTER EIGHT

Jasmine watched Adam from the doorway of his bedroom with an indulgent smile. "How many times do you need to go over those papers? Your dad says they look good."

Adam turned and stared up at her with sober whiskey colored eyes. She walked into the room, closing the door behind her.

"What is it?"

She stood near him, taking in his black wavy hair, the tips brushed against his shoulder, and angular face similar to his father. Silas' genes overpowered hers leaving his mark on all four of their kids. Adam and David's light brown eyes were the only concessions given her in their features. Even Jackie and Renee were feminine versions of their father.

"Timing. Is this the best time to live over there? I mean with everything going on here."

"Like what?" She asked surprised at his question.

He stood, dwarfing her five feet, six by several inches, and moved to his closet. Opening the door, she saw three suitcases stacked on each other. Unsure what that meant, she glanced at the luggage. "All packed?"

"For a few days, now. That's the problem. I can't shake the idea that now isn't the right time. Maybe go next week or later until it feels right." He moved his hand in a circular motion around his chest. "Inside. Right now," He shook his head. "Something feels off."

"Follow your gut, wait until you believe the time is right." She leaned in and kissed his cheek.

"That's what David said last night. He cornered me asking questions while I was with Tangela on the patio." He looked at her. "Seriously, when is Sarita coming home?"

Jasmine sighed and wrapped her arm around him. "When she's ready. Asia said she's enjoying the internship, learning new languages and meeting people. Best time to travel, see the world is when you're young." And single, unmated, she left off.

"Do you wish you'd done more traveling when you were younger?"

She squeezed his waist and released him. "Yeah, I do. But that wasn't my path and I wouldn't trade that time for anything. Rone and Reese are worth it all. Plus, now I get to see the world with the love of my life, so I'd say waiting, for me, was a sweet deal."

Once the kids were in high school, Silas surprised her with three trips a year, anywhere in the world she wanted to travel. Together, they visited historical landmarks, often with Angus and Shyla or her mom, Victoria, and Jacques. Traveling with men over 300 years in age made the history in Egypt, Africa, Pacific Rim and China come alive.

"Where's Tangela?" Jasmine asked about his current girlfriend. Most pack members didn't date. If two people liked each other they got together, no labels. But not her pups or their friends. They watched human TV and picked up pop culture from teenage shows and the internet. Setting a new trend, most of the students now labeled their relationships causing all kinds of problems with jealousy and insecurities. Fights over relationships had gotten so bad, Silas spoke to the students about it. Since Adam and Renee had girl or boyfriends, the talk didn't have much staying power.

"Home, she'll be here later to watch a movie and hang out," he said. "Talked to Jackie a couple days ago, she's going to Tennessee to visit Nionis. Have you talked to her since she's been there?"

Jasmine thought back over the past two days. She had been extremely busy preparing for a party she was hosting for the women who worked in her network. "No I haven't. I'll call her later tonight."

"Good, I can't reach her."

"What do you mean? I thought the four of you stayed linked all the time."

"We do but it's not, what's the word? Intrusive. Otherwise we'd never have privacy. It's like a partial block," he explained.

"You tried to reach her and she didn't respond?" Jasmine asked to be clear.

He nodded. "Happens at times. Especially when I'm with my girl or hanging with the fellas. She'll get back to me when she has a moment, that's what I do."

Easygoing Adam was not disciplined like Jackie who never dabbled in abstracts. Life was a huge puzzle for Jackie. One she never grew tired of exploring and revealing various layers. Serious about family and work, Jackie wouldn't have ignored Adam's call this long unless something was going on. Something Jasmine didn't know about. She tapped her pocket. "I'll give her a call." She opened the door and stepped into the hall. "Is Tomas waiting for you or will he go ahead?"

"Waiting. We're going together when we go. In the meantime, he's hanging out with Matt's family in Cincinnati until I'm ready."

Jasmine nodded.

Tomas couldn't be around Renee since they broke up. Davian said his son was devastated and had a hard time letting go. Renee buried herself in work at the gallery but still lived here at the compound. There was no way to avoid seeing each other if he remained in town. Waving goodbye, she headed to her private suite. Inside she looked at the wall clock to calculate the time. It wasn't that late, but it was possible Jackie was asleep.

She called Renee instead.

"Ma, I was going to call you," Renee said answering the first ring. "I don't think Tomas and Adam should leave right now. If you can get Sarita back here, in the compound that would be a good idea."

"What's going on?"

"Earlier in the gallery I overheard three male humans discussing unrest in the area where Tomas plans to go. I tried to call him, but couldn't get through. I don't have a good feeling about this."

"Have you talked to your dad?"

"Security told him after I had them listen and check out the guys. Hank did a scent scan, and ran them through some database. These guys live in a smaller country near Russia and shouldn't be here," Renee said.

"Near Russia? They spoke English?" All four kids spoke several languages but Renee had the best ear.

"No, but Hank taped them and ran it through a system for Daddy."

"Chances are he's talked to Hawke but I'll contact Asia so Barticus can keep our girl safe," Jasmine said worried about the repercussions if anything happened to Sarita. Not only would Barticus, Sarita's grandfather and Europe's Alpha, set the area on fire, but Asia, her closest friend and her mate Hawke, would grieve deeply over the loss of their daughter.

"Tell David," Renee said.

Jasmine closed her eyes, took a seat and tucked her legs beneath her. "You haven't told him?"

"No. I don't want to do it."

"Adam had a bad feeling and delayed his trip so no worries there. I'll have your dad tell David," Jasmine said, thinking of Sarita being in harm's way with that area of the world being unstable. "I need to talk to Asia. I'll call you later."

"Okay. Mom!"

Jasmine exhaled. "What?"

"You called me, what did you want?" Renee asked.

"Oh, have you talked to Jackie today?"

"Yes, earlier today. She and Nionis went sightseeing, helicopter ride over the mountains. She sounded relaxed but having fun. I suggested she take a few more days off."

Preoccupied with Asia and Sarita, Jasmine accepted Renee's explanation. "Okay. Talk to you later."

Sweet Bitch?"

Jasmine blew a stream of air. *I need to talk to Asia about Sarita."*

Barticus is handling it already. Sarita has been moved to Barticus' den with Amynta and their pups."

Have you told David?" she asked.

No but I will since you don't want to. Adam's delay proves both he and his beast have matured. I'm happy he listened and changed his plans."

She hadn't thought of that. *"You talked to him? Told him what was going on?"*

Yes, just now."

Good. Renee talked to Jackie, seems she's having fun."

Tango, her personal security bumped into his mate while they were in Gatlinburg. It was a good day all around. Theron is pleased and sent a replacement," Silas said.

Adam said Jackie didn't get back in touch with him."

She talked to Renee?"

Yeah, a few hours ago, when they got back to Nionis' place."

Maybe she's treating him like he treats us, responding after he's done everything else," Silas said in a dry tone having been on the receiving end of Adam's delayed responses many times.

Jasmine laughed. *After my nap, I've got a conference call with a few of the women coming to the party. Wake me in an hour."*

The door opened and Silas stepped inside, closing the door with a snap. "Before you take that nap I'd like to show you something." He pulled his shirt over his head and grinned at her.

CHAPTER NINE

Holding both small pups' hands, Jackie and the others walked into a large stone and wood building ablaze with lights. A man with splashes of white in a head full of dark hair, stood at the door waving them inside. His dark eyes assessed her and each person entering.

"Welcome, I'm Ramos. Come inside, I've got food if you're hungry, a warm bed if you're tired and a sturdy chair if you'd like to talk. Come in, you're all welcome," Ramos said with a slight Spanish accent.

The child tugged on her hand to get her moving faster as if the offer would be repealed. She quickened her steps and headed toward the smell of food. Her stomach rumbled as she entered a room with a long wood table and several chairs. The boy pointed to the covered dishes on the buffet.

"Hungry?" She looked beneath the covers and glanced at him. Beneath the bright lights, she got her first good look at eyes similar to her brother's light brown, an unruly mop of wavy, reddish-brown hair and skin a few shades darker than Nionis. He nodded so hard, a hank of hair fell onto his forehead. Smiling, she took a plate, put small portions of everything and placed it on the table in front of him. Nionis and another female entered the room.

63

This is Marsha; she's the one who told Ramos and Antwan about the clinic. The big guy's Antwan, Ramos' mate. They own this place. It's a sanctuary for runaways, Nionis explained through their link.

Jackie didn't respond. "Do you want the same thing I gave him?" She asked the other child who hadn't responded to anything so far. Just as thin, but taller than the other boy, his dark brown eyes appeared haunted. Freckles dotted his nose and upper cheeks on his pale skin. Dirty, stringy, black hair touched his shoulder, covering mottled bruises on his neck. When he didn't answer, she prepared a similar plate, took him to the table and had him sit.

"Can you check him?" She asked Nionis when the child didn't move.

"Hello, I'm Marsha," the teen said moving to the table with a plate. She sat across from Jackie.

"Hi, Marsha, I'm Jackie." She looked up at Nionis, stood and went to get her a plate while Nionis did her thing with her eyes.

No one fully understood how or why Nionis saw things no one else could. Her dad and Matt, the doctor at the compound both checked Nionis and found nothing. But over the years her gift of sight had proven invaluable in helping KnightForce, the Special Forces of the Wolf Nation, solve certain cases.

One draw-back, the gift didn't work all the time. That's why Nionis only volunteered information when she had it, asking her to check the child probably wouldn't give them any information.

Ramos entered the room with another young girl behind him. She filled a plate and sat next to Marsha.

"This is Penny," Marsha said when Jackie sat next to Nionis.

"Hello, Penny," Jackie said smiling at the pretty girl.

Ramos sat on Marsha's other side with a cup of coffee and watched Nionis who held the silent boy's cheeks between her palms.

Anything? she asked Nionis.

"What are you doing?" Marsha pointed to Nionis.

"He hasn't spoken or responded to anything since he left the clinic. I'm looking to see if it's physical or mental," Nionis said in a matter of fact tone.

Jackie bit into a piece of savory chicken and waited for Ramos' reaction. He didn't say anything.

Nionis dropped her hand, rubbed the child on his head and kissed his cheek. "It's going to be okay," she murmured. "His name is Sean. He saw his family... what happened to them."

"They would've killed him," Marsha said. "If he remained like this, not talking or eating, he would've been left behind to die or shot."

Jackie's gaze flew to Marsha, whose sympathetic gaze rested on Sean. "Who would've killed him?"

"We'll discuss that later," Ramos said smoothly. He looked at Nionis. "Can you reach him? Coax him out enough to eat?"

Nionis looked down at the child. "I'll try." Taking his chin, she drew his gaze to hers.

"What were you doing at the clinic?" Marsha asked Jackie. "You're too old to go there."

"Old?" Jackie smiled, stalling for time.

Marsha grinned. "That's not what I meant. It's just not normal for grown-ups to be there, that's all."

"My friend." She pointed to Nionis. "Had a, let's say vision or premonition that she needed to be there. I went with her."

"She gets those a lot?" Marsha asked watching Nionis' stare down with Sean.

"It's all relative. I've known her most of my life, so in that regard no. But lately, yes, she's had them a lot."

"Is she normally right when she has these?" Marsha asked.

"Yes." It didn't escape Jackie's notice Ramos allowed this conversation but stopped the one on killings. Looking at the children at the table she understood why.

"Would you like more, little one?" Ramos asked the small boy who finished his food.

"No." The boy pushed his plate away, scooted from his chair, walked to Jackie and raised his arms.

Smiling, she lifted him into the chair next to her. "I'm almost done eating." He nodded and relaxed into the chair.

"You have experience with young ones," Ramos said with a grin.

"Yes, lots of relatives with pups," she said after taking a sip of water.

He nodded, his gaze on Nionis and Sean.

"How are the other two, the ones who were unconscious?" Jackie asked remembering Antwan and Quinton carrying bodies.

Ramos sighed. "I'm not sure. Quinn's working on them. One may be beyond his abilities, or anyone's."

Jackie disagreed. Matt was the best doctor in the nation for half-breeds and her father, could repair the beast in half-breeds and full-bloods. Should she reach out for help? She wasn't sure. Rescuing pups was awesome but could the operation be improved, made more efficient? She needed more information, as pieces of the puzzle formed in her mind.

"Quinn's a doctor?" she asked. Surprised they allowed a human to work with the pups or on the grounds.

"Yes, he finished school, never took his boards," Ramos said with a bit of pride that made her wonder if he knew Quinn's family personally.

She nodded and looked around. "Where do we put the dishes?"

Ramos' smile widened as he pointed to a closed door. "The kitchen is through there. If you placed them in the dishwasher I would appreciate it much."

Jackie turned to the small boy who dozed in the chair next to her. "I will be right back, I'm going to put our dishes away."

His eyes rounded as his gaze flitted around the table. When she stood, he scooted off the chair and followed her. Jackie held out her hand to take Penny and Marsha's plates as well.

"Thanks," Marsha said handing her both plates.

Jackie looked behind her at the small boy and walked into the kitchen. It was larger than the one in her mom's private suites but smaller than the main kitchen in the compound. Two dishwashers book-ended granite covered island in the middle of the room. A large walk-in freezer and separate refrigerator stood side by side. Pleased they were equipped to feed large amounts of people, Jackie rinsed and placed the dishes in the washer. Maybe the ranch was legitimate. She hadn't seen anything to the contrary but it wasn't optimized and that bugged her.

"What's your name?" she asked her small companion hoping he would tell her this time.

"Craig." Yawning he raised his arms.

"Alright Craig, time for bed." She lifted him and returned to the dining area. "Everyone, meet Craig. He's sleepy." Her gaze met Ramos, who nodded.

Marsha and Penny stood. "This way," Marsha said walking from the table.

Jackie glanced at Nionis and Sean. When the boy nodded, Jackie thanked the Goddess Nionis had broken through his pain and communicated with him. *I'll be back,* she told Nionis.

Okay, " Nionis said.

Down the long hall, a set of stairs led up to a level with several doors. Marsha pointed to a door. "Sean's the only other boy at the moment. He can sleep with us or in his own room."

"Yesterday, two boys were reunited with their den," Penny said, surprising Jackie.

"That's wonderful. I'm sure they were happy," Jackie said as another puzzle piece fell into place.

"Doesn't happen often," Marsha said. "But when it does it's really good... if the den's a good place." She glanced at Penny and then at Jackie.

What was that about? Jackie wondered.

"He's sleeping already," Penny pointed at Craig. "He can sleep with me so he won't be alone. It's hard being alone." She walked to a door, opened it and stepped inside.

Jackie followed. The pastel colored room held two queen sized beds, two chests, two desks, a large floral rug on hardwood floors and paintings of flowers on the wall.

Cozy.

Penny pulled back the covers and slid into bed. Jackie didn't push the teeth brushing or face washing rituals she and her litter-mates grew up with. Instead, she lay Craig on the bed, took off her half boots and got in beside him. Marsha sat on the other bed watching.

Craig curled into her. Penny pulled the covers over them and scooted closer to Craig in the middle. Within a few minutes the two were sound asleep, snoring lightly. Jackie listened to Craig's breathing, and worried about his future. What happened to the pups who weren't reconnected to their dens? How could Ramos support this kind of operation? Why didn't Alpha Gilbert know about the ranch in his territory? Were Ramos and Antwan a different type of rebel? What about Quinn?

Quinn.

Swallowing hard, she closed her eyes to shut out the vision of him driving, walking, talking to others and his scent. Earlier at the clinic, she'd lowered her control on her beast. Quinn's scent slammed into her and lodged in her chest making it difficult to breathe.

What the hell? The man didn't say two words to her after she refused to get out the truck. The truck? She exhaled as the enormity of her unprecedented actions tonight rolled over her.

What in the name of the Goddess possessed her to get into the truck in the first place? Renee would think she, Miss Logical Extraordinaire, had lost her mind. She hadn't calculated risks, or possible outcomes. No, like some inexperienced ninny, she'd hopped into a stranger's vehicle, without security riding point, and refused to leave.

A tidal-wave of possibilities rolled over her. She discounted the notions that she'd been hypnotized or hoodwinked by Nionis especially since she'd jumped in the vehicle before her friend. No doubt Nionis would have questions about that later. Maybe seeing the children hurt and being taken pushed buttons she hadn't realized existed. Raised in a home with high walls and sophisticated electronics for protection kept her and her siblings safe from what these children suffered but that didn't stop her feeling of kinship.

All her life she learned pack came first. Victimized, Craig, Penny, Marsha and the others hadn't experienced true pack ethics and that disturbed Jackie on a visceral level. Exhaling, she accepted that line of reasoning for her erratic behavior. It fit. Made logical sense. At ease, she rose from the bed, picked up her boots and left the room in search of answers. Jackie hadn't realized the teen had left the room.

Marsha sat in a chair with a book in the hall. She put the book down when she saw Jackie and stood with a smile. "This way." She turned, and headed for the stairs.

Jackie wondered at Marsha's role at the ranch. Was she involved with Quinn? Why did she think that? The idea caused her throat to tighten and stomach to clench.

It wouldn't be right for these men to become involved with any of the pups at the ranch. The pups were too vulnerable to say no; besides it would be changing one abuser for another. Although she didn't know Ramos or Antwan, Quinn's clean scent cleared him of debauching pups. By the time, they reached the dining area, Jackie was prepared to question the men's motives for taking in the pups. Ramos and Antwan sat at the table holding hands reminding her of their mated status, canceling her questions. Mates didn't, couldn't cheat.

Nionis and Sean sat across from them eating.

"He's eating," Marsha stated the obvious and left the room with a softly spoken. "Goodnight."

Everyone waved, or said goodnight as she left.

"Good," Sean said around a mouth of food. "Really good."

Retaking the seat next to Nionis, Jackie noticed how tired her friend looked. *"You okay?"*

A little. Nionis took a sip from her glass. *It worked. I was in control, going in, searching, looking for the little boy in the shadows of his mind. For the first time, I'm beginning to understand this thing I've had all my life.* She met Jackie's gaze. *I should have gone into psychology instead of sociology."*

Jackie leaned into Nionis, and gave her a gentle bump. *No school could've taught what you learned tonight."*

Nionis smile crept up her face until it reached her eyes. *"True. Plus, this probably only works on dual-natureds, and I don't need a degree to work with pack. Not with something like this,"* she corrected.

Jackie wondered how Nionis had been able to read Quinn at the restaurant but decided to hold that conversation later.

"What do you say, Nionis?" Ramos asked.

Nionis straightened.

Jackie wondered what she had missed and watched the two men.

"The job on campus is important, I can't leave right now. And I agree it's not a good idea to come and go from the ranch often. Why not call me in when you have a case similar to Sean? I'll come and work with them, help you in any way I can."

"Or you can assist in processing on the front end," Antwan said.

"Each pup?"

He nodded. "Tonight's not the norm. Although we can house up to 25 pups at a time, we've never done that. Typically, we get a pup every two months, sometimes three or four months pass without any pups."

"What happens when the pups aren't reunited with their den?" Jackie asked.

"We train them to survive on their own and place them with dens when they're ready," Ramos said, his gaze flit between her and Sean.

Jackie nodded and lapsed into silence while processing this new puzzle piece. If pups were being placed with dens there would or should be records. She doubted Ramos registered the half-breeds in the national database which her brother, Tyrone, managed. How did these two know the quality of the dens they placed the pups in?

Sean scraped his plate and offered Nionis a timid smile. "All gone."

"Good pup. Time to sleep." She looked at Jackie. "Where's Craig?"

"In bed with Penny." Jackie pushed back her chair. "I'll show you."

Nionis stood, picked up their plates.

"Go ahead, put him to bed, we'll clean up here. Come down when you're done, I know you have questions." Ramos looked at Jackie as he spoke.

"Thanks," she said glancing at the clock on the wall. It was after four in the morning. They needed to get back home or call in their absence to their parents soon or all hell would break loose.

Quinn looked at the young half-breed on the table and cursed. He hadn't been able to save her. By the time they reached the ranch she had already lost a lot of blood. According to the nurse at the clinic, bleeding after her miscarriage had been the reason the child had been dropped off at the clinic by some shadowy person the nurse claimed not to know.

Since the half-breed wasn't responsive at the clinic, Antwan hadn't wanted to move the girl, but Quinn wanted to try. Despite the odds of success, he had to try. Within 30 minutes of arrival at the ranch, she died. His second loss in 10 years. "Sons of bitches," he cursed beneath his breath. Another life snuffed too young. She hadn't had a chance to live, to see much of the world. Where was the justice in this? Rage rolled through him as he stared at her unmoving on the table.

A whimper from the other bed drew his gaze.

Quinn tamped down his anger, and checked the equipment on the other girl. Same age as Marsha, but in her second trimester. Strong vitals, but her litter was in distress. He looked at the sonogram images again. Three pups moved, one didn't.

It might come down to the mother or her litter, he hoped not, but it would take a miracle to keep all of them alive. His stomach growled, he looked at the clock. Almost four in the morning. After making notes regarding both patients, he rechecked the equipment. A few moments later the pregnant pup, eased into sleep. Quinn left the basement and went upstairs to grab a bite.

When he entered the dining room, his uncle and Antwan sat alone at the table looking at each other. *Hungry?*" his uncle asked through their link.

Quinn nodded, lifted the covers and frowned at the near empty platters.

"It'll just take a moment to fix you something," Antwan said standing.

Replacing the covers, Quinn headed into the kitchen. "Cereal's fine." He grabbed a bowl and the container of cereal.

"Are you sure, it'll just take a few minutes to make an omelet, I have everything ready to go," Antwan said firing up the burner.

Quinn poured milk over the flakes in his bowl. "Thanks, that sounds good." Bowl and spoon in hand he headed into the dining room, sat across from his uncle and ate.

"It's not your fault," his uncle said into the silence.

Quinn didn't respond.

I've asked Nionis to help as a consultant."

Quinn's spoon halted halfway to his mouth as he met the older man's gaze. "*The chatty one?*"

Ramos smiled. *I suppose. Although if there was something of interest to the black haired one, she'd talk as well. Antwan said she refused to leave the truck, almost dared you to argue with her.*"

71

Quinn snorted but didn't take the bait. He had nothing to say about the stubborn woman with a soft spot for vulnerable pups.

You don't mind about Nionis? His uncle pressed.

Quinn shrugged. "*This is your place, your decision who comes, goes.*"

Nonsense, his uncle snapped. *I want your opinion.*"

I don't know enough to have an opinion, Quinn answered honestly. *Just met her in town less than 24 hours ago. She asked too many questions.*"

Were you human deep?"

Quinn nodded.

Yet she knew you were dual-natured, his uncle said.

I suppose, her questions leaned in that direction, Quinn said thinking back.

She has a gift that allows her to see, which is why Antwan allowed them to come."

See what? Quinn leaned back as Antwan placed the omelet filled with meat and cheese in front of him.

Different things. Ramos declined an offer for an omelet. *She worked with Sean.*"

Sean?"

Ramos explained what happened an hour ago at the table. Just as he finished, Nionis and Jackie re-entered the dining room. Ramos stood. "Let's all go to my office as the walls are fortified for privacy. I believe we'd all like plain speaking," he said watching the ladies.

Tired, Quinn wasn't sure he wanted any part of a long conversation, until his gaze met Jackie's. Beautiful with a touch of steel and vulnerability. She looked confident, yet bewildered, a temptingly strange contradiction, impossible to resist. He took his dishes into the kitchen, placed them in the dishwasher and followed everyone into his uncle's study.

Inside, Jackie and Nionis sat in his uncle and Antwan's two large, overstuffed leather chairs forcing the two men to sit on the long sofa on the other side of the room. Which left the chair at the desk as the only other available seat. Quinn opted to lean against the wall to watch.

"First, I'd like to welcome you ladies to the ranch," Ramos said and then launched into the history of the place, his ancestry and the people they helped over the years. Quinn glanced at the wall clock and hoped the old man would get to the interesting part like what were these two doing alone at night without those security guys?

Jackie asked a few questions, which his uncle or Antwan answered. Quinn stifled a yawn and tried to follow the hum of the conversation but exhaustion chased him.

"Quinn?" Antwan said. "Can you answer her?"

"What?" he said straightening against the wall.

Antwan pointed in the direction of the women. "She asked what happened to the girls we carried to the truck?"

"Who asked?" He looked at both women.

"I did," Jackie said, her voice and gaze challenging.

Reminded of his failure, his gaze steadied on hers. "I don't know names, but one died."

Jackie's hand flew to her mouth.

Nionis gasped.

Quinn explained the girl's condition when they arrived at the clinic and what happened after they arrived at the ranch. "The other is on support." He explained her condition and the problems she faced.

"Can you get help for her?" Jackie asked. "Maybe take her to one of the hospitals, see if they can do something."

Quinn wondered if Jackie understood the ranch operated beneath the radar and was unsanctioned in the pack. La Patron's lackeys would turn them in before he could ask for help. On the flip side, if the girl and the lives of her pups could be saved, it might be worth the risk. "I'd be open to looking into that," he said slowly looking at his uncle. "If they can help save the mom and her pups I'd go that route in a heartbeat."

"I may be able to help," Jackie said. "Tell me how much can be said to keep this place safe, what you're doing is too important to risk."

Quinn's gaze swung to meet her determined one. For a few seconds, they stared at each other assessing.

"On one condition," Ramos said.

"What?" Jackie asked looking across the room at his uncle while Quinn continued watching her.

"Allow your beasts to breathe, both of you have been human deep too long."

Jackie stood pointing at Quinn. "But he's human."

Stunned by the accusation and surprised by his uncle's demand. "She's not human?"

CHAPTER TEN

Jackie stared at Quinn. "You're a breed?"

He stiffened and moved from the wall. "Half-breed, yeah. You?"

Confused, she shook her head. "Same. But I thought you were human."

"You were supposed to," Quinn said. "Just like you wanted me and any other dual-natured to think you were human. Not many of us can go that deep into our human side to fool full-bloods."

She refused to answer the question in his tone. Instead she looked at Ramos. "Are you his sire?"

"I'm standing right here," Quinn snapped.

Jackie met his aggravated gaze. "Just asking."

"Ask me," he said.

"Is he your sire?" she asked crossing her arms across her chest.

"No. What were the two of you doing at the clinic without your security guys?"

"Security?" Ramos said looking at Nionis.

Jackie glanced at the clock. They'd need to sneak back home before Chip realized the house was empty. Plus, she would need to talk to her boss again. Helping these pups was more important

75

than returning to work. She hadn't worked long enough for vacation but that didn't matter, he could terminate her but she would make sure the pregnant pup got the help she needed.

Nionis waved. "My sire's overprotective."

"But you live on pack lands," Antwan said watching Nionis. "You should be safe there."

Nionis shrugged. "I agree but it's not my decision." She glanced at her watch. "I used a blocker that prevents anyone from listening to my conversations and makes it seem like we're inside, but that won't hold once the sun rises. We need to get back." She looked at Quinn. "Can you come to the house later this afternoon to discuss arrangements for your patient. It'll be hard to return here and we'd like to help."

Jackie wondered if Quinn would refuse their assistance.

"Yeah, sure. If we can save them I'd be grateful," he said in a humble tone. "Excuse me, I need to check on her and prepare the other for burial." He glanced at Jackie and then met Nionis gaze. "Leave your information with Antwan. I'll contact you when I'm on my way." He walked out.

"He's not my biological son," Ramos said. "But he's my son all the same. My sister died when he was a pup and I raised him as my own. Smart, compassionate and loyal to a fault. A man, or woman, won't ever find a better friend or companion than Quinn. If you wrong or hurt him, his memory is long and he's makes a formidable enemy. Because of our lineage, there are depths to him he hasn't explored," Ramos said watching Jackie.

"Lineage?" Nionis said scooting to the edge of her chair. "Who's your mam? Sire? We could be related."

Ramos nodded. "It's possible. Arianna bred hundreds of pups over her lifetime. She may hold the record. My sire was an alpha long dead. He fought a challenge for Arianna and lost. The new Alpha bred several litters from her until he was challenged and lost. It was a vicious cycle back then mated pairs were rare." He glanced at Antwan and smiled.

"Did full-blood pups hate breeds back then?" Nionis asked.

"No. We were raised as pack with no differentiation." Ramos paused and looked at his mate. "Someone has to point out differences for pups to notice them in a den. This hatred, and divisiveness is taught."

Jackie agreed. At school and in college she made friends with both full bloods and breeds without those being issues. When she didn't get along with someone, typically their personalities clashed or they were assholes.

"True, I saw that in college," Nionis said standing. "A few full-blood jerks called me names, tried to put me down. But there were a lot of half-breeds at the school which nullified the haters." She yawned and stretched. "Need to get to bed." She looked at Jackie and then Antwan. "Can you take us back to town?"

Antwan stood. "Yeah, be right back with the keys."

Ramos joined Nionis and placed his hand on her shoulder. "Your purpose is clear to you?" he asked.

"Not crystal, but better than before. I'm glad the pup was returned to his den, that's great news."

He nodded. "Now to keep Penny safe from Taurus. He's a tricky one."

"The rebel leader?" Jackie asked walking closer to them.

"Yes." He explained the rebels plan for the child.

"That's disgusting," Jackie said. "How could her parents give her away like that?"

"You're thinking with your human side," Ramos chastised gently. "Half-breed rebels shun their human side, their wolves dominate. In their minds, it's an honor for their Alpha to mate with their pup."

"That's not mating," Jackie said.

"Not in the mate for life sense, like Antwan and myself. But to build and fortify the pack, the sexual act for that purpose is never rape, but mating," he explained.

"She's too young," Nionis said. "She should be in school." Nionis followed Antwan toward the exit.

"Many don't have that choice," Ramos said. "Families outside the pack don't receive the bounty pack offers."

Confused, Jackie touched Ramos shoulder, drawing his attention. "Why are they outside the pack? I don't understand."

"In every society, there are those who seek their own path. In this great nation, many humans live outside the boundaries of their government every day. They hide, live off the grid, survive off the land. They aren't in the databases that allow services their government provides. Can they walk into a soup kitchen for a free meal? Yes. But their government doesn't provide those. Wolves need pack, they don't need a large or a nationally structured pack. For some, living with three other wolves is sufficient without following national rules. Understand?"

"Because they don't want to serve La Patron their pups lack basic education?" Jackie had a hard time believing that.

Ramos shrugged as they continued to the truck. "For some, that's the way it works, who can say what makes a man do the things he does."

Jackie agreed and sat in the back seat while Nionis and Antwan sat up front.

"Until we see each other again," Ramos said waving good-bye.

"Bye, nice meeting you," Jackie said watching him return inside. The drive into town was quiet. Tonight had been an eye-opener. Did her parents know about rebel villages? She doubted it. Children in this area needed health care and schools. How do you help people who chose to become invisible? Uneducated, isolated and with no hope they were perfect breeding grounds for rebel propaganda. Perhaps it was time to re-evaluate how to win against rebels. Obviously, her father, the Alphas and KnightForce missed something.

Pieces of this much larger puzzle tumbled around her mind. There were too many unknowns to find a solution. She needed more information. The truck stopped next to Nionis' car.

"Thanks, Antwan," Jackie said stepping out.

"You're welcome, we'll see you soon. Craig and Sean will demand it." He waved and drove off.

Nionis opened the car and they slid inside. "Chip's going to be pissed."

"Yeah. Think he'll report it to Theron and Gilbert?" Jackie asked before yawning.

"Oh yeah. Prepare to be grilled by our parents later today." Nionis started the car and pulled onto the road. "But I wouldn't change a thing," she said a few minutes into the silence. "For the first-time things clicked in my mind and life. It's mind-boggling-awesome."

Jackie smiled and hugged the giddy feeling of doing something that made a difference in the life of someone else.

Working on the rebel problem from this level energized her in a way working at the Pentagon or corporate America never had. "I hear you. The pups are so cute, we have to help them without getting Ramos or Antwan in trouble. I don't want the ranch closed down."

"Agreed. So, what do we say?" Nionis glanced at her.

Jackie thought about it for a few minutes. "I can't lie to Mama, she'll read through it and then be hurt. Daddy could search my mind for the truth anyway."

"You can't block them from what you don't want them to know?" Nionis sounded surprised.

"Never have. I could try." She thought for a few seconds. "How do I do it?"

"Think of a wall and build it brick by brick around Ramos, Antwan, Quinn, the ranch and the kids. Everything from last night place it in a box or brick jail that only you can open. Go inward and focus on locking away that information."

Eyes closed, Jackie saw all the people from the ranch. In her mind, she waved them into a room and locked the door behind them. A click sounded in her mind. She waited a few seconds. "How do I know it worked?"

"I'll search through our link," Nionis said. A few seconds later she smiled. "Good job. Not a sign of anything from the ranch." She held her hand out toward Jackie who slapped it and watched the sun rise.

"So where have we been all night?" Jackie asked.

"With some guys we met," Nionis said.

"Really, that's the best you've got? Mama won't believe it. Daddy neither. Renee most definitely won't."

"They'll believe it if you say you went with me to make sure I was okay and nothing happened, that kind of thing. It skirts the truth. We were with some guys we met, Craig and Sean if they need names."

Jackie laughed which turned into a yawn. "That's more than skirting the truth."

"We have to think of a way to help that poor girl," Nionis said in a soft voice. "Matt could help for sure."

Jackie bit her lip. "We could say we found her, or that your vision led us to her."

"That might work since I've found people before. Quinn would need to move her to another place, a hotel maybe and we could pick her up from there. Chip could put her on a plane and take her to Matt."

"What about Alpha Gilbert? Won't he be offended we didn't take her to a pack hospital here in Tennessee?"

"Probably. Daddy would," Nionis said. "I'll check out the local pack hospitals."

"I could call Gem, get a referral," Jackie said thinking of Asia's daughter-in-law who was a doctor in a Florida pack hospital.

"That might expedite things, just don't tell her what Quinn said, then she'd know the child had seen a doctor and my visions aren't normally that precise."

"Got it. When I wake from my nap, I'll make some calls. Are you going to contact Ramos about our plan?"

"Yeah, we've linked so I'll bring him current," Nionis said.

"What? You linked with him already? What about your den's information?" Jackie had a hard time relating to Nionis' carefree attitude about life. Mental links were personal and intimate.

"I've been blocking people from my thoughts since middle school. Ramos knows nothing about me I don't want him to know. His guesses are fairly accurate, though. I think he and I have similar gifts. I'm going to look up his family line, see if there's a connection."

"I don't want anyone to know about my family, Nionis." Jackie made sure her friend understood how serious she was about her privacy.

"I know. If they find out La Patron's your sire, it won't be from me. You can check me through our links. I have a lot of mental storage boxes on lock-down. So far no one's broken through and many have tried."

"I appreciate it," Jackie said looking out the window. "We share a lot, Renee and the boys, and I don't want anyone to access that."

"It's locked away, Jackie. You and I are linked and I've never seen anything about your family. I think it's instinctual to shield private matters in our minds. What I suggested by locking things down is an extra measure of protection," Nionis explained.

Jackie nodded as they pulled onto Nionis' street. Chip and another male Jackie hadn't met stood in her driveway with their arms crossed watching them pull in.

"Shit," Jackie whispered when Tango walked out the garage.

CHAPTER ELEVEN

Quinn hadn't been on pack lands in several years and took a moment to really look around. Well maintained homes lined the streets. Healthy, happy kids ran around playing tag, climbing trees, laughing. The stark contrast of the healthy pups in this community and the ones seeking refuge at the ranch pained him. He pulled into Nionis' driveway and turned off the engine. Grabbing the small bag Antwan sent for her, he stepped out his vehicle, looked around the neighborhood again and walked toward the front door.

Nionis opened it before he reached the covered porch. "Come in, come in." She waved and stepped aside. Inside the cool interior, he handed her the bag and looked around.

She laughed while looking inside the bag. "Tell Antwan thanks for returning my tracker." She tossed the bag onto a small, wooden end table. "Come on, Jackie's back here."

He followed her through a hall into a larger room with a flat screen television, chairs and a low coffee table in the middle. Jackie sat on a long sofa reading through a stack of papers. She looked up at him and smiled. "How's it going?"

"Good, thanks." He sat on the chair opposite her and looked at three white erase boards on the table.

"Feel like watching a movie?" Nionis asked. She wrote yes on one of the erase boards.

"Yes, sounds great as long as it's not mushy or horror. Something action packed, James Bond like if you have it," he said smiling at her frown.

"Grease is my favorite movie," Nionis said surprising him when the title flashed on the screen.

A musical? Seriously?

She held up her board so he could read her new comments. "Get over it. We need to get to the hotel."

Quinn nodded. By now his uncle should have the pregnant teen in the motel near Knoxville along with two of his trusted helpers watching over her until Quinn and Nionis arrived. The plan seemed solid. He picked up a board and wrote. "Okay. Whenever you're ready."

Nionis nodded and pointed to Jackie.

Jackie wrote. "I'm good, let's go. Chip should be done verifying everything by now."

Quinn frowned as he read her comments.

Nionis shook her head. "Explain later, let's go."

They stood and strode outside. He took one last look around the neighborhood as Jackie and Nionis entered his SUV. No one was surprised to see a car pull out after them. Quinn pretended to get directions to the motel from Nionis, making a few wrong turns and arguing with her to make it appear more authentic. When they arrived at the motel, Nionis jumped out the car first and headed to the stairs. Jackie and Quinn exited a few seconds behind her and watched Nionis' performance. Holding her head, she walked slowly past each door, doubled back once and then knocked on the door Ramos had given her.

No one answered.

Quinn, Jackie, and two security guys stood outside the door as Nionis turned the doorknob. It didn't open. Nionis spoke to the tall, slender man behind her. "Chip, open this door. I know you sense it too. Someone's sick in there."

Chip glanced at Quinn who stood a good distance from them, human deep. Assuming, Quinn was human, Chip turned the knob until it broke and pushed open the door. Nionis strode in.

"She's pack," Nionis said. "Get the van here for her now!"

Jackie ran inside, leaving Quinn behind since pack security wouldn't allow him to follow. An unmarked medical van arrived within10minutes. Impressed, Quinn watched from the corner of the doorway as the paramedics examined the girl and announce her pregnant condition. Jackie and Nionis were upset that the child was pregnant and sick. They demanded she receive immediate care.

The paramedics ran tests in the motel room and within minutes announced the same conclusion it had taken Quinn 30 minutes to make. Having the right equipment made all the difference.

"Can you fix it?" Nionis asked the paramedics.

"I've sent the information to the hospital, once the doctors examine her I'm sure they'll be able to give her the help she needs." The paramedic lifted the girl in his arms and walked down the steps with her, similar to how Quinn had done last night. Stepping aside, he watched them put her inside the van and drive away. Nionis and Jackie walked out behind the paramedic and waved Quinn over.

"Let's go." Nionis threaded her arm through his and they walked ahead of Chip and the security team. "There was no identification on her so we need to follow them to the hospital."

"Why?" Quinn asked knowing Chip was listening. "You said you had a feeling something was wrong, and you were right. Why do you need to do more?" Hospitals made him uncomfortable and if he could avoid going he would.

Nionis glanced behind him and then looked at him. "You're right. I just need to be sure I got this one right. It's important to me." She looked behind her at Jackie. "Tell you what, you and Jackie go on to the house, I'll have Chip bring me there after we check on her. Won't take long."

Stunned, Quinn stared at her to see if she was serious. Splitting up like this wasn't a part of their original plans. He waited for Jackie to step in and get them back on track. Instead, Nionis spun and ran toward the car that followed them from her home. Jackie walked over to him appearing just as clueless over what they were supposed to do now. She glanced over her shoulder. "I guess we should get moving. Maybe grab a bite to eat on the way," she said.

"Okay," Quinn said slowly wondering what was going on. He and Nionis weren't mind linked so he couldn't ask questions. Instead he asked his uncle if he knew what Nionis was doing. Ramos claimed she hadn't told him about this part and suggested Quinn play it by ear.

He unlocked the SUV for Jackie and slid into the driver's seat. She pulled on her seat-belt and pulled out a small black device. After pressing a button, she looked at him. "I'm really hungry but if you're not, it's okay. We can just go back to the house and wait for Nionis."

CHAPTER TWELVE

"No, food's a good idea." Quinn pulled out the parking lot and headed to a small family owned restaurant he enjoyed. Jackie continued tapping keys on her phone during the drive. He turned on the radio and smiled when one of his favorite songs, I can't stop loving you by Ray Charles played. Humming with the music, he turned onto the road leading to the restaurant.

"You like that?" Jackie asked when the song ended.

"Yeah, he's got a nice voice. I've got most of his music." He didn't bother asking if she liked Ray Charles, her surprised expression over his response made it highly unlikely.

"Nionis' brother sings all of Ray Charles music perfectly. If you closed your eyes you'd swear Mr. Charles was in the room singing."

Mr. Charles? How old was she? "Hmm, I doubt I'd be fooled. I've seen several of his performances over the years, have a few autographed albums and been collecting his music for a while."

She chuckled. "His number one fan and a snob."

"On all things Ray Charles, yes." He grinned and pulled into the parking lot. "They have really good food here." He slid out the driver's seat and was on his way to open the door for her when she stepped out the car. Together they headed inside.

"Hello Quinn," Ms. Jones the owner called before she walked into the kitchen.

He waved and took a table near the back overlooking the parking lot. Once seated he pulled the laminated menus from behind the napkin dispenser and handed her one. "Everything's good, you won't go wrong with anything you choose." He glanced at his menu and replaced it.

"What are you ordering?" Jackie asked looking at her menu.

"Liver and onions."

She grimaced but didn't look away from her menu. "I don't see that."

"It's not on the menu. I always ask for it and she cooks it for me."

Jackie's brow rose. "Sounds like you're spoiled."

He laughed.

She glanced at him and shook her head. "You do. I'll have the ribeye and fixings."

"Me too." Pleased she ordered his favorite meal.

"What? No liver?" she teased and he appreciated her sense of humor.

"Not today. Today I need a slab of beef. They cook it just right here." He looked around the restaurant. "Where's your security?"

She shrugged.

"Had a chance to look at the menu?" Ms. Jones asked, placing two glasses of water in front of them.

"Yes. Two rib eyes and fixings," he said.

"Cooked the same?" she asked, glancing at Jackie.

"Yes, that'll be good," he said.

"What's the same?" Jackie asked looking at Ms. Jones.

"Done on the outside, red inside. He likes it a special way, took us a few times but we finally got it right." She winked at him.

"That'll be fine, then," Jackie said.

Ms. Jones chuckled as she walked off.

"You don't trust me?" he asked watching her.

"Nope. Not with my food."

He smiled." Got it. Never order for you."

She nodded.

"Why do you need security? Nionis said her dad's a state Alpha but won't say which one, so I get why he'd have security on her. Is your father an Alpha too?" He wanted to know more about this beautiful woman but wasn't sure why.

"I don't want to talk about it," she said surprising him. "How long have you lived with Ramos and Antwan?"

"A long time. Where do you live when you're not visiting friends?"

"Texas. Have you always lived in Tennessee? She asked.

"No. Louisiana for a while. Do you have siblings?"

She paused. "Yes, three. Do you have siblings?" She took a sip of water but continued holding his gaze.

"Not anymore." He slammed the door on the death of his parents and litter mates at the hands of rebels. "Did you guys get in trouble this morning when you arrived home?" He'd wondered if the security guys discovered they had slipped out last night.

She grinned. "It was reported we slipped out but Nionis has a special gift and is granted leeway. They tagged your car, so they know where we are. Plus, we have to keep trackers on us at all times."

He frowned. "So, you won't be returning to the ranch?"

"Probably not. I don't want to do anything that would put you guys at risk."

"What about Craig? He was crying for you this morning." Quinn didn't want her to feel guilty over bonding with the pup, but the idea of her not returning to his home bothered him. Since he couldn't explain why he felt that way, he latched onto Craig's early morning response.

"I'm so sorry," she said and he sensed she meant it, which made him feel worse for using the pup. "We'll work something out. I don't want him to feel abandoned."

"Abandoned? After spending a few hours together?" Quinn needed to backtrack this whole idea of Craig needing to see her. The pup quieted once he realized she had to return home. Ramos had the entire matter under control.

Straightening in her seat she glared at him. "Traumatic hours. His entire world was turned upside down. Those memories last longer than normal, everyday ones. So yes, abandoned."

He held up his hand and shook his head. "Whatever." When Ms. Jones delivered their platters of ribeye, home fries, corn on the cob and home-made rolls he breathed a sigh of relief into the silence.

"Thank you," he said taking his knife and fork.

"This smells delicious like my mama's cooking," Jackie said.

Ms. Jones' smile widened. "Enjoy. I'll check on you later." She walked off humming.

For the next few minutes neither spoke, unintelligible moans of delight rose from their throats as they polished off their meals. Done, he smiled at her empty plate. "Dessert?"

"If it's as good as this was, definitely," she said.

"It's better," he promised.

Jackie watched Quinn as he passed the menu to her again. When she looked at the homemade desserts and thought of her mama's delectable baked goods. It wasn't often but sometimes she'd go into a baking jag where she filled the counter-tops and table with cakes, pies, cookies, danishes, breads and pastries.

"Suggestions?" she asked although she planned to take two slices of the red velvet cake back to Nionis' for them later.

"Pound cake sundae is my favorite."

"Ice cream, chocolate syrup, nuts, whipped cream and a cherry on top of a slice of 7-up cake?"

He nodded. His eyes were lit like a pup's first run. "No whipped cream or cherry, though."

"So far you've batted 100. I'll have that too, plus a couple slices to go."

When Ms. Jones returned for their plates, Jackie placed their dessert orders. She met Quinn's amused gaze and smiled. "When did you go to med school?" She had wondered about that since discovering his training.

"A long time ago. I passed the human board registered under a different name. Uncle Ramos doesn't count them as the real certifying agency."

"I see." The bias against humans and dual-natureds went as deep as breeds and full-bloods in some areas. "What schools did you attend?"

He shrugged. "I don't want to talk about it." The gleam in his eyes said he would be as recalcitrant as her.

"That's fair." She wasn't accustomed to small talk with strange men. Typically, she discussed work or military strategies or business matters.

Ms. Jones placed their desserts on the table. His smile brightened as he looked up at the older woman and Jackie wondered if anyone had ever looked at her in that manner. Certainly not with the near reverence as he looked at that tasty dessert, not that she wanted him to gaze at her that way, she clarified.

"Thank you, this makes my day," he told the owner.

Ms. Jones giggled.

Jackie blinked. The woman had to be in her 60's and she stood there giggling over Quinn's, gooey, sincere words.

"You always say that," Ms. Jones cooed, tapping Quinn on the shoulder. She glanced at a stunned Jackie. "He's a sly one. Enjoy and I'll bring your to-go desserts in a few minutes." She left their table with Quinn moaning after his first bite.

"She warms the cake just enough so the ice cream melts, the buttery taste, it's damn good," he said chewing slowly and licking his lips.

Instead of eating, Jackie watched him eat scoop after scoop, licking his lips and moaning. The sounds he made went straight to her head like a fine wine, intoxicating her. Tingles pooled in the pit of her belly at the sight of his tongue on the spoon. His spoon stopped midway.

"Try it." He waved his spoon toward her untouched bowl.

Without leaving his gaze she dug in, pulled out a scoop and ate. Chocolate syrup on top of cold vanilla ice cream, plus the warmth of the cake, all the flavors burst on her tongue. Understanding dawned as she also moaned in delight and licked the chocolate from the spoon. Eager for another taste she savored every spoonful until the utensil hit the bowl.

Stuffed, she looked at Quinn to ask how often he ate here.

The hunger in his gaze stripped the question from her mind. She glanced at his bowl, it was half-full. "What?" she asked unsure what to say.

He shook his head. "You know how to eat, um, ice cream," he said in a husky tone. He took another scoop of his and within a few moments was done.

Shaken by his heated gaze and the dark timbre of his voice, Jackie pushed away her empty dish. Nionis was right, Quinn was interested. She inhaled and released it slowly. Why did knowing that make her nervous? He wasn't the first man to show carnal interest and wouldn't be the last.

Ms. Jones placed a plastic bag on the table and the check.

Quinn dug in his pocket, pulled out a small roll of cash, gave her a large bill and a smile. "The rest' s for you." He winked.

She took the cash, check and smiled. "Thanks, Quinn, come back soon." She smiled at Jackie and left.

"You're ready?" Quinn asked looking at his watch.

Where did he need to be? She wondered at his rush. "Yeah."

Walking out the restaurant, they waved to Ms. Jones and headed to the car. Just as Jackie placed her hand on the door handle, two full-bloods raced at her.

Quinn leapt forward, kicking one in the back, sending him flying past Jackie, face-down he skidded across the pavement and rolled over holding his shredded face. Jackie moved lightning fast, jumped and landed feet first on the full-blood's chest, knocking the breath from him. He grimaced, and bucked to knock her off balance. Jackie dug the heel of her boot into his chest and pulled the small blade from her pocket. Gasping for his next breath, the full-blood stilled as she moved aside, bent forward and placed the blade against his neck.

Quinn ran forward, jumped and kicked the other beneath the chin, lifting him before sending him jetting backward. He hit a sewer concrete riser with a loud thwack, and hit the ground at an awkward angle. She winced, knowing it would take time for his back to heal even if he shifted. Quinn glanced at her, nodded and headed back to the restaurant.

The full-blood beneath her blade growled. The air around them warmed. "You shift out here, you die," she whispered and pressed the blade drawing blood. Her stomach recoiled at the sight of blood rolling down his neck but as long as she kept the blade in place, he would continue to bleed.

Grunting, he clamped his lips tight together while writhing beneath her hand. The skin on his face re-knitted over embedded gravel and dirt causing more pain than the blade at his neck.

"What the hell are you doing attacking us like this in front of humans?" she said close to his ear. When he didn't speak, she leaned forward, and growled in his ear. "I will rip you apart and toss you in the damn creek if you don't talk now." She slid the knife deeper into his neck.

He yelped. "You took our pups, we want them back," he huffed.

Rebel. She looked at Quinn who talked down an angry and upset Ms. Jones who wanted to call the police. *Nionis?"*

Almost home."

Two full-bloods just attacked." She explained what happened and wanted to know if they should contact KnightForce or the Alpha or local pack security.

Be there in a minute,' Nionis said after getting their location. Sure enough, Nionis, Chip and an unmarked van arrived at the restaurant within five minutes. Chip lifted the rebel who'd hit the concrete riser. He hadn't moved since he landed. Another security guy grabbed the one Jackie had been holding. Chip nodded with an approving grin at her blade as he walked by.

Nionis looked at each rebel before they were loaded into the back of the van.

Ms. Jones watched the van drive away with a worried frown. Whatever Quinn told her replaced the frown with a smile. Seconds later she strode inside the building and Quinn walked over to meet them.

Chip watched Quinn with curiosity.

Jackie suspected Chip realized there was more to Quinn.

"Ready?" Quinn asked Jackie after greeting Nionis and Chip.

Nionis hid a smile and returned to Chip's vehicle.

Chip watched Quinn and Jackie until they were in their vehicle before returning to his own.

Once they were on the road, Jackie looked at Quinn. Those rebels weren't the only ones who underestimated his fighting skills. Living in the compound, she had seen the best of the best in the Nation practice and compete. Quinn could definitely hold his own with any of them which surprised her. He'd remained calm, level-headed and handled the threat immediately. "How'd you sense them?" It bothered her she was so human deep she hadn't picked up on the threat until he flew past her.

"Practice. I train breeds to be human-deep but still aware. It's second nature now."

"Teach me," she said without thinking. A bad habit she had around him.

He nodded. "Okay. Did he say why he attacked?"

She repeated what she learned.

"Looks like I'll be trading this truck in," he said after a few moments. "I'd like to meet you."

"What?" she said confused.

"Breed to breed. I'd like to meet you if you don't mind."

Unsure if that was a good idea, Jackie tried to think of a reason to say no and couldn't find one. "Okay, but only while we're driving. Once on pack lands I'll put them back up."

He nodded. Moments later she smelled his beast.

Her beast leapt in her chest, she flew forward, almost hitting the dashboard.

Quinn's truck swerved.

Horns honked as Quinn pulled off the road onto the shoulder. Taking gulps of air, he looked at her. His eyes had lightened to a coffee creamed brown. A sheen of sweat and an incredulous look covered his face.

"What's wrong?" she asked in a breathy voice trying to control her beast. "I'm having a hard time holding her in." Scared she'd need to call her parents for help she pressed her stomach, closed her eyes and counted. His scent wrapped around her head. Tiny pinpricks penetrated her skin. What the hell?

"Don't move," he growled.

She glanced at him holding his head in both hands. "Human deep too long?" she asked wondering if this was what Ramos meant.

He groaned. "No. It's you. Your scent is... my beast wants you... I want you. It hurts holding back."

Jackie stiffened as his words worked a weird magic. Shaking her head, she opened the door and stumbled out. "No," she whispered and took a large gulp of air. The need to submit to him lessened but thrummed beneath her skin. Rubbing her suddenly chilled arms she took a step from the car.

Nionis!" she called out.

What's going on? Why are you on the side of the road?"

93

Jackie looked up as Nionis and Chip pulled up behind them. Happy to see her friend, Jackie fought against her beast to move toward Nionis' car.

Nionis and Chip stepped out and moved toward them.

Fangs bared, Quinn jumped out his vehicle and growled at Chip.

Nionis held up her hand with a slight smile. "Stay back Chip, he'll kill you and no one will blame him."

Hands up, Chip stepped back.

Confused, Jackie's head whipped from Quinn, to Chip who returned to the driver's seat, to Nionis. "What're you talking about?"

"You released your beasts?" Nionis asked in a soothing tone, watching Jackie and then Quinn who walked over to them.

It took everything in Jackie not to rub against him, he smelled so damn good. Quinn wrapped his arm around her waist, pulling her against him. They fit perfectly.

"Yes," Quinn said, his voice rubbed against her skin like smooth velvet.

She throbbed low in her belly.

Nionis' smile widened. "Great. Now you know what Ramos and I suspected. You guys are mates."

"What?" Jackie yelled.

CHAPTER THIRTEEN

"Mates?" Quinn whispered. The word caught in the air, drifted high and settled around his shoulders. *Mate!* His beast agreed. Internally, everything clicked. His initial attraction to her. Allowing her to hijack his mission. The burning desire to see her again today. If nothing else, the unrelenting hard-on from watching her eat ice-cream should have told him she was different.

Hands on her shoulders, slowly, he turned her to face him, lifted her chin with his finger and lost his train of thought in her cerulean hued eyes. "Mates."

Confused, uncertain, tempted, all those emotions flashed through her gaze as he leaned forward to taste her. Their touched lips set off a firestorm of exquisite need. Heat, desire, need, and crazy lust crashed through his chest, destabilizing him for a few seconds. Hunger replaced gentleness. His grip tightened as he plundered her mouth to satisfy his innermost craving to be a part of her.

Desperate to get closer to his skin, Jackie wrapped her arms around his neck pulling him closer. Liquid heat blazed through her at his taste, and delectable scent. She needed to get closer. His hand gripped her hip. For some insane reason that inflamed her.

Raising her leg, she moaned in his mouth when he lifted it rubbing her against his hardness.

They broke apart gasping for a few seconds but it was too long. Grabbing his hair, she kissed him while lifting her other leg. Grabbing her ass, Quinn lifted and placed her achy core against his cock. Legs wrapped around him she continued tasting him, searching for secrets, losing herself in his scent.

"*Jackie*," Nionis called from a distance.

A part of Jackie knew she should stop, but a new, unknown part of her couldn't let him go. Not yet. She and her beast liked his scent and taste too much.

Nionis tapped her shoulder. "*Stop. Ease up. You're on the side of the road; people are slowing down to watch.*"

Quinn pulled pack, breaking the connection.

Breathless, Jackie rested her forehead on his chin. "*Goddess, this... this is crazy. I can't get enough of him. I'm burning inside for him. Never happened before,*" she told Nionis. Fire raced through her limbs. Everywhere he touched itched, ached for more. Thirsty for his taste, she licked his chest. He groaned as his fingers dug into her hips, holding her tight.

It's okay, we need to get the two of you someplace safe where you can finish this," Nionis said.

Tell Quinn what to do. I'm not...can't think clearly right now," Jackie said as Quinn released her legs one at a time, holding her close while she steadied.

"Quinn, I'll drive your car and Chip will follow me. You two sit in the back and do not, I'll say it again, do not have sex while I'm driving. Wait until you get to the house." Nionis paused and pointed at them. "Say yes I understand."

"Understood," Quinn said his voice a deep rumble in his chest. Arms wrapped around each other, Jackie and Quinn slid in the back seat leaving no space between them.

Nionis started the car and pulled onto the road. *We got approval for you guys to stay at the safe house.*"

Huh? Why?"

Because you're not human deep and La Patron has a thing about his pups being exposed to everyone without a ton of security. When you're human deep it's not an issue but I'm thinking, you can't shut down your wolf right now, which means everyone on pack lands who's ever been near La Patron will pick up his scent through you."

What?" Jackie tried to focus as Quinn placed kisses all over her face and neck distracting her.

Never mind. When you get to the safe house have fun with your mate. No one will bother you or recognize your scents. Call me later."

Yeah, okay," Jackie whispered as Quinn kissed her while squeezing her breasts. Zings of pleasure raced between her legs.

"No sex," Nionis yelled as Quinn unsnapped Jackie's jeans.

He placed his palm at the juncture of her thigh and rubbed.

On fire for him, Jackie moaned and drew his face between her palms, pulling him close for another kiss.

He growled and pulled her on his lap.

"Goddess help me survive this," Nionis muttered.

Jackie dropped her forehead against Quinn's and took several deep breaths. "We need to wait."

"How much further?" Quinn asked.

"Less than five minutes I promise," Nionis answered quickly.

"This... you...it's incredible," Quinn whispered as she pulled his face against her breast. "I've never needed anything or anyone like I need you right this minute. It's like everything I've ever done, or all roads in my life led me to you, to this point." He scoffed. "Makes no sense I know but that's how it feels, inside." He tapped his chest with two fingers.

Jackie took those fingers, kissed them and pulled his arm around her waist. "When I can think straight again, I'll try to figure it out... can't help it, that's just the way my brain works."

"I like your brain," he said before pressing a kiss against her breast. "Sexy brain." He kissed the other breast. "Sexy woman." He kissed the spot between both breasts.

"Goddess you smell so good," Jackie whispered running her fingers through his thick dark brown hair.

"We're here," Nionis said in a loud, relieved voice as she hit the brakes.

Quinn fixed Jackie's shirt in place and made sure her pants were buttoned before lifting her to the other side. Cautious, he opened the door and slid out. Inhaling, he turned noticed security guards in the distance but not too close. Certain the area was safe, he extended his hand to his mate and assisted her out the car. He didn't recognize this place.

"Where are we?" he asked Nionis as he and Jackie stood wrapped in each other's arms looking at the brick one story building.

"Safe house," Nionis said. "With the rebels following you to the restaurant, we don't want to take chances and I didn't think you wanted to wait and go back to the ranch."

"No," Jackie said pulling Quinn's hand and heading to the front door. "This is perfect. Thanks Nee."

"You're welcome," Nionis said starting the car.

Quinn waved goodbye, opened the door, and scanned the place. Sensing they were alone he picked up Jackie and walked inside.

"*Don't forget the real reason you're at the safe house,*" Nionis cautioned. "B*e careful or your mate may not live to sire your pups.*"

Jackie blinked away the sensual fog as Nionis' outrageous words sent a chill down her spine. Her father and mother would be seriously pissed if something avoidable happened because they were lax on security. But neuter Quinn? Goddess, that didn't bare thinking about. *How many guards are watching this place?*" she asked Nionis while allowing Quinn to pull her toward the first open door off the hall.

Five but you're La Patron's daughter, who knows how many will be enough? Just do what you need to do and go human deep when you can, Nionis said and disconnected.

"Did you check security?" she asked Quinn just as he opened the door.

"Not really." He turned, ran toward the door they entered, and locked it. He left and went to the back. She heard the clicks of locks engaging and leaned against the wall smiling. Her mate was being thorough she thought as another door opened and he walked down.

Jackie wondered what was in the basement but decided to wait and ask rather than investigate on her own. A few minutes later she heard his footsteps.

"Thanks for reminding me to re-check security." He took her hand, turned and headed back down the hall.

"Where are we going?" She looked back toward the bedroom door and then at his back as they entered the large eat-in kitchen.

"Basement, top notch security. Best of all I recognize it and was able to put in my code to activate it." He stepped into the stairwell, waited for her before closing the door and activating the alarm. Smiling he took her hand and walking in front of her, led her further into the basement.

"It looks better and bigger than upstairs," she said looking around at the comfortable living area with a large flat-screen TV, gourmet kitchen that put the one upstairs to shame, gaming area and three large en-suite bedrooms. Jackie didn't see much, Quinn's long strides had them inside a coral and cream bedroom. With the slam of the door behind them she was back in his arms.

The fire of need had been banked while they saw to their safety, but it was a long way from extinguished. Her arms wrapped around his neck as the kiss deepened. Moaning she pulled at his shirt, needing to feel his skin. They pulled apart gasping. He pulled his shirt over his head and tossed it to the ground.

Had she really thought him human before? The fire behind his dark brown eyes made them a lighter, sherry color that no human she'd ever seen could match. Muscles rippled across his chest and arms as he toed off his shoes and shoved down his jeans.

"Off." He pointed to her reminding her to stop watching and get naked. Eager to be with her mate, Jackie unsnapped her jeans, pushed them down and off. Unbuttoning her blouse, she sensed his gaze and took her time with each button. When done, she dropped it to the ground, reached back, unsnapped her bra and let the strap dangle from her finger. Smiling she looked at him. Her beast yipped and howled from the force of his arousal.

"Come here," she said dropping the bra and placing a finger beneath the elastic band of her panties. "I need a little help getting this off."

Quinn moved so fast she hadn't finished the last of her sentence before he lifted her in his arms, turned and fell on top of her on the bed.

"Tease your mate?" He growled clearly fighting his beast for dominance.

"Can you control him?" She didn't mean to be insulting and for many that question would be an insult but they were mates. She needed to know early on how he handled his beast.

His lips quirked. "He thinks I'm going too slow no matter what I say, he wants us inside you, claiming you."

"All that to say, what? You've got this?" She bit his earlobe.

His long claw ripped her panties.

She smiled and lifted so he could get them off.

"I suppose that's what I'm saying." Lying between her legs he pushed them apart while staring at her. "You're so damn beautiful. I'm the luckiest breed in the world."

He didn't mention pack. The thought slid across her mind and disappeared as his finger slid inside, stretching her. Wiggling slightly to get him where she needed her thoughts centered around the pleasure he wrung from her.

"Tight. Sweet," he said after sucking his finger. "Mine." With that one word, he thrust forward.

Jackie bucked and froze at the intrusion.

Quinn stopped. "You okay?"

How do you admit you'd been with a boy you barely felt, but now, being with a man, the stretch, the burn, and the hurt? "Give me a minute." She inhaled and relaxed as her body adjusted, accommodated his much larger girth.

Resting on his forearms, he remained fully inside her without moving. "Take your time, I'm not going anywhere."

Once the burn lessened she did a tentative hip roll.

He groaned but didn't move.

She rolled her hips and lifted slightly.

He groaned again but didn't move.

Sensing he wouldn't do anything until she gave the okay, Jackie relaxed further. She placed her hands on his ass and rubbed his firm cheeks. Their gazes met. His need and desire for her lit another fire in her, inflamed her confidence. She wrapped her legs around his waist, pulling him down.

"Ready?" she asked.

He lifted slightly and slid back into her. "Always." With each thrust her need for him grew. She bucked and tried to move faster. He followed her lead, picking up the pace, thrusting deeper, watching her, always watching.

100

"More," she gasped sensing something just beyond her grasp. "Close."

He drove into her, hard and deep, shoved up her knees. "Wait for me, I'm close." Fast. Faster thrusts. Eyes closed she rose higher and higher. Higher than she had ever been. She hadn't known this level of bliss existed. She cried out as pleasure tore through her. Body shaking, she couldn't wait another second as she flew apart. His shout and shuddering above her announced they had both reached their peaks.

CHAPTER FOURTEEN

Silas sat back in his chair and stared at the large green, blue and white abstract picture his daughter, Renee, made for him while in college. It seemed just yesterday he held each of his pups in his hand, naming them with hopeful expectations. For the most part they all surpassed anything he could've imagined. His one complaint, if it could be called that, was none of the four seemed interested in remaining in West Virginia at the compound. His building of the art museum in Charleston was proof of how far a father was willing to go to keep his pups near.

He ran his hand through his hair to shake off his melancholy mood. "*Jasmine?*"

Yes?"

Where are you? I need a word." He stood preparing to meet with her.

I'm here, walking to the door of your office." The outer door opened. He heard her speak to Rose before opening his door. Dressed in brown pin-striped fitted trousers with matching brown boots, and a short sleeve cream shirt she looked delectably polished with her hair pulled back in a bun

Inhaling deeply, he allowed her scent to fill and warm him. He extended his hand. She took it and he enfolded her in his arms.

His beast eased as she rubbed his back in silence while sending waves of warmth through their link.

"Jackie met her mate."

Jasmine stiffened and tried to pull away. He held her close. "What? When?"

"An hour ago. It's the young pup, I had Jacques researching."

She eased into his embrace. "The one with Tango's mate? From the restaurant?"

"Yes. Seems they were both human deep and didn't know."

"What changed that?" she asked.

"I don't know. The report came from Gilbert's security guy, the one assigned to Nionis. He was in the car behind them."

"Where was Jackie's security?"

"We're looking into that. I think there was a mix up but won't know for sure until later."

For a few moments, he just held her. "She's too young to be mated."

Jasmine chuckled. "Really? Seems like Rone and Rose mated close to this age."

"So, is this it? Twenty? Is that the age where mates know each other?" he asked wondering how the rest of his pups would take the news.

"I don't know." She paused. "Jackie hasn't contacted me, or Renee I'm guessing. Wonder how she's handling it?"

"It?" he growled suspiciously.

"Mating heat. If it's as strong--"

"Stop. Spare me the image of my princess and someone I cannot find one iota of information about mating."

She rubbed his chest while grinning. "Your princess is becoming a queen, Wolfie. Another man will have the top spot in her life."

"That I don't mind, as long as he's a good man."

"Is there a man good enough for your princesses?" She asked in a sly tone.

He slapped her ass and tugged her closer. "Impertinent."

"Accurate assessment you mean."

"Not really. My wolf's aggravated because her mate is a mystery and isn't in our system."

Jasmine stilled. "What do you mean not in the system? He's not a rebel or something like that is he?"

"I don't know who the hell he is and that pisses me off." He released her waist but held onto her hand. "Who is Quinn York?"

"Other than your son-in-law I don't know," Jasmine said softly reminding him of his daughter's mated status.

"This can be a disaster. A rebel? You're the only reason I haven't had Gilbert or the Tennessee KnightForce get involved." He looked down at her. Read the compassion in her gaze and released a stream of air. "How do you want to handle it?"

"Wait for her to contact us. It's what I would want if it were me. When she contacts us with the news we'll deal with who he is at that time. Remember, this mating thing goes both ways. He has to accept her and we're part of the deal."

Silas snorted. "You're sure about that?"

She squeezed his hand. "Yes. Family is important, we raised them that way."

"I'd give up everyone to be with you," he said softly.

"You were raised differently, Silas. I'll bet she tells her sister before 24 hours passes. If Renee doesn't do something I'll be surprised. My guess is she'll go check the guy out and no, we won't ask her any questions or interfere with their relationship. Jackie will tell us when she's ready."

"You have a lot of faith in them." Being wolf he wasn't as sure as his mate over how his pups would respond in a mating situation.

"I've been through this with Rone and Rese. When you teach children the importance of family, they don't forget. Stop worrying. If ... what's his name?"

"Quinn."

"If Quinn is the man the Goddess or whoever assigns mates, has for Jackie, then we need to support them not make it harder."

He leaned back and stared at her. "You're not upset? You're ready to give our daughter to a stranger? And unregistered person, which is against our laws by the way."

"What happens if Jackie refuses her mate?"

Silas heard Jasmine's frustration but refused to give in, this was too important. "Breeds can walk away, she doesn't have to mate with him."

"No, but it'd be painful for her." She paused. "What's going on with you? Why am I defending pack policy? If it was another pack member would you react this way?"

"Maybe. He's unregistered, Jasmine. A law-breaker, someone who's against rules I created. I know nothing about him, that's the issue here."

"Okay, as long as it's not you wanting to hang on longer to your princess," she muttered.

"No. Well that may be part of it but there's a larger picture. What does he do when he learns she's my daughter and he's a lawbreaker?"

"What if Jackie knows he a lawbreaker and hasn't turned him in?" Jasmine countered.

Silas hadn't thought of that but knowing Jackie, he'd say Jasmine was right.

"If she hasn't turned him in it's for a good reason. At some point we need to trust our children's judgment as they go into the world," Jasmine added.

"How does that look? What message does it send that my pup allows lawbreakers to go free? It sets her up as judge, which she's not authorized to do." He shook his head. "This can of worms shouldn't be opened. I need to put a stop to it before things get worse."

Jasmine crossed her arms, meeting his gaze with fire in her eyes. "I hope you're not going to interfere with Jackie and Quinn's mating."

"Not directly. We need to know more about him, learn if he poses a threat," he said trying to make her understand.

"First off, if Jackie's mate is a threat to pack, we'll deal with it at the appropriate time. Like I said the bond goes both ways, he can't hurt or deny her either. That connection puts us in a better position to find a way to fix a problem."

Desperate, Silas spoke his fear. "What if he takes her away, hides her somewhere?"

Her brow rose along with an inelegant snort. "Is there a place on the earth I can't find my kids? Or you?"

A knot in his chest eased. His mate was right. As Alpha and sire, he could find his pups anywhere. Maybe Jasmine had a point and his reaction wasn't rational.

"Plus, Jackie's not weak. No man can put her in chains and keep her from what she truly wants. To think that's a possibility is an insult to the woman who raised her," Jasmine said firmly. "Once the mating frenzy eases up, she'll be able to think clearer. Don't do anything that will damage our relationship with either of them, Silas. I mean it."

Silas read the steely determination in her gaze and ran his hand through his hair. "Okay. You're the expert on family. You say the family bond will over-ride pack mentality to cleave to your mate."

Jasmine rolled her eyes. "That's not what I said."

Pleased he'd goaded her out of her anger, he smiled. "I'll back off for now. Jacques will continue searching for information on the pup, and I'll have Gilbert's security give them space. Will that make you happy?"

"Yes." She paused. "When David finds out, will he stay or go find Sarita?"

Silas had wondered about that. "I think he'll look for her to see if they're mates."

Jasmine nodded. "Renee and Tomas?"

"I never thought they were mates, Renee needs a stronger wolf than Tomas. They'll reconnect to verify that for themselves."

"I liked Tomas. He supported Renee's passion for art, and she put down her paintbrush to watch him play sports. For her, that spoke louder than words," Jasmine said.

"True. But I never thought it was love, gratitude maybe." He paused and then grunted. "A picture of Quinn York's been uploaded. Want to see?"

Jasmine nodded and moved to look at the monitor on his desk. Silas pulled up the screen and stepped back. Much taller than he expected, the pup's dark hair and eyes could belong to any wolf. "Half-breed." Silas pointed to faint outlines of a tattoo beneath the short sleeves Quinn wore.

"Handsome," Jasmine said. "He and Jackie look good together." She pointed at the next picture with Nionis' back to the camera. "He's much taller than her. She doesn't seem to mind his rebel status or the way he's holding her."

Silas saw the pup's arms around his daughter's waist and grunted again.

106

Jasmine's gasp at the next picture and then delighted squeal aggravated him to the point he turned off the monitor.

"What's the matter, Wolfie? You didn't like seeing your princess kiss her prince?"

CHAPTER FIFTEEN

Jackie rolled over, her feet tangled with Quinn's. Opening one eye she glanced at the clock on the nightstand and winced. Almost six in the morning. She moved slightly toward the edge of the bed, removing Quinn's arms and legs. Goddess had they been at it all night? Her stomach grumbled.

Hungry and naked, she got out of bed and headed to the bathroom. Flipping on the switch she shook her head in remembrance of what they'd done in this room last night. Or was it yesterday afternoon? She couldn't remember. After taking care of her immediate needs, she turned the shower as hot as it would go, and stepped inside. The heat eased her abused muscles and washed away most of Quinn's scent. Smiling, she wondered what he'd say about that.

"*Sorry about yesterday*," her sister Renee said through their link.

Yesterday? Jackie had no idea what Renee meant.

We were supposed to talk about... never mind, you don't remember so I take it back. What's going on? When are you going back to Texas?"

Texas?"

Your job, house, car all that stuff you were excited about, although... it sounds like something's changed. Spill. What's going on?"

Jackie stuck her head beneath the shower. *One sec washing my hair."*

That's all you'll get. I'm hip to your stall tactics. I'll wait."

Grumbling at her annoying sibling, Jackie grabbed the shampoo and conditioner to wash her hair. Yesterday's conversation with Mr. Bradley resurfaced. He hadn't been happy when she explained she needed time off and suggested he release her from her duties. He suggested she take the rest of the week and they talk again at the end of that time. She shouldn't have agreed but he sounded so hurt and disappointed that she would quit that she let it go and promised to talk to him soon.

When she was done, she wrapped towels around her hair and body. Looking in the large bathroom mirror she searched for signs of what? Being mated? Maturity? She blew out a breath, unwrapped her hair and worked on the tangles. *I met my mate and we've been getting to know each other."*

Ha ha. Very funny. Try again."

Jackie hadn't realized Renee wouldn't believe her. But given the problem with the others not knowing their mates she should have expected it.

Wait, Renee said in a soft voice. *You don't joke about things like that. Seriously? I mean you met him? It's a guy, right?"*

Relieved she wouldn't need to prove anything, Jackie shrugged. *"Yeah, I told you about him. Quinn."*

The guy you met in Tennessee? The one Nionis said liked you?"

Yeah, turns out she was right."

But he's human."

Jackie heard her sister's confusion. *Human deep."*

Get outta here. For real? Renee said. *He's a breed?"*

Yeah. He's amazing."

"I'll be there later today."

That snapped Jackie out of her romantic fog. *"What? Why?"*

To meet him."

Frustrated by Renee's answer Jackie put down her comb. *Again, why?"*

Because you're my sister, to welcome him to the family and to make sure he understands he has to treat you right at all times. It's called an inspection."

He's my mate, your inspection won't stop fate," Jackie said picking up her comb.

I know, but I'm still coming. Question, do I tell Mama and Daddy or the boys or should I keep a lid on it?"

Jackie shook her head and closed her eyes. She wasn't ready for reality to intrude. Renee would come whether she agreed or not, chances are she'd do the same thing if their positions were reversed. But her parents? How would she explain him not being in the database? Plus, Quinn had no idea who she was; they hadn't gotten around to it. *"I'm not ready to share him or whatever this is we have."*

For a few moments, Renee didn't say anything. *"Okay. After I meet him I'll hang with Nionis' a bit."* She paused. *"What's it like?"*

Jackie heard the hope and excitement in Renee's voice reminding her of the time when she asked Renee the same thing about her first kiss with Tomas. *Let's just say I understand why Mama and Daddy still go at it like rabbits."*

Specifics, Renee demanded.

Literal fire runs through you at his touch and it's always there beneath the surface. You're always hungry for more of him and his scent... it makes your panties wet."

Wow, really?"

Yeah and he's the only one who can help. Otherwise the need just grows and grows. I can see why it's hard to survive without your mate."

It's half-living."

Jackie grunted her agreement and worked on the other side of her hair.

Damn, I didn't feel that with Tomas. He was good, but nothing like what you're saying. Renee sighed and Jackie's heart went out to her. *I guess he's not the one."*

Your mate's out there, when you least expect it, you'll meet him," Jackie said praying to the Goddess her words were true.

Yeah, you're probably right. Anyway, I'm sure David will go after Sarita once he learns about this. Don't keep it a secret too long."

Jackie hadn't thought about that and the possible repercussions for others. *"Good point, I'll call Mama later today."*

After I arrive. Uncle Angus came home this morning on the jet so I can leave here in an hour and should be there after lunch. Go ahead and eat without me. I'll let you know when I make it to Knoxville."

"Okay. Love you."

"Love you, and I'm happy for you. Mama's going to be ... really happy."

"Daddy?" Jackie said in a dry tone.

"Depends on your mate, 'Renee said. *"Believe me he'll be thoroughly researched."*

Jackie's heart clutched. In the other room, Quinn's feet hit the floor. *I'm sure. Listen, I'll see you later."* She disconnected and waited to see her mate in the light of a new day.

Bare chest and ass, Quinn strode into the bathroom and hit the water closet. Washing his hands, he met her gaze in the mirror and smiled. "Thank the Goddess, yesterday wasn't a dream." He shook the water from his hands and dried them with a paper towel as he walked to her. It took everything within her power to hold his gaze instead of looking at his incredibly long, thick, cock.

"I'm sure I've done nothing in life to deserve you as my mate but I'm grateful to the Goddess anyway." He took the comb from her and drew it through her springy curls. "Beautiful." Their gazes clung as he repeated the process of combing her hair, something no one other than her parents, nurse and sister had ever done.

Sister. Okay, she needed to tell him. "Um, my sister's coming today."

"She is?" His gaze never left hers as his hands massaged her scalp and neck.

"Mm hmm, that feels great," she murmured.

"How many sisters do you have?" he asked.

"Just the one. Litter mates," she added.

"Brothers?" He moved to her shoulders.

"Four, two are litter mates."

"Are you mentally connected to them? Your litter mates?" he asked.

She nodded. "Yeah, since nursery."

"Nursery? Interesting name, your mam's human?"

Jackie wasn't sure if now was the best time to get into this but since he'd opened the door and she sucked at lying, she'd walked through. "Yes, a breeder."

His hands paused for a few seconds and then continued. "Breeder, not half-breed?"

"She doesn't shift, can't mind-speak with us, just my sire and one other person, she's a breeder." Jackie didn't understand why his questioning her understanding the difference between the two bothered her but it did.

"Sorry, just surprised. Ramos' mam was a breeder. It's just odd to meet someone with the same experience that's all."

She turned and looked up at him. "How many have you met?"

He gave her a crooked smile. "Other than Ramos and now you, none. I mean I know they're out there, I just haven't met any others."

"I'm surprised your sire and mam aren't coming, are you close with them?" He took her arm, starting at the top massaged her muscles.

"Yes, we're close, I haven't told them. What about you? Have you told anyone?" She wasn't ready for the "my dad's La Patron" conversation.

He grinned. "Just Ramos when I told him I wouldn't be returning last night. He wasn't surprised. Nionis had already spilled the beans. She may have told your parents too."

Jackie shook her head. "Not a chance."

He paused and looked confused. "Why'd you say it like that? Are your parents going to give us a hard time? Not approve or something?"

"My father will want a full background check on you," she said watching him.

Quinn frowned. "He won't find me, I'm not in the system." He glanced at her. "Should I enroll so he can investigate me?"

She thought about it. It might work but her dad would still have questions.

"I was joking," Quinn said into the silence. "But you were thinking it over. Jackie, if I go into the system I can't help Ramos anymore. I wouldn't be able to come and go to help the kids at the ranch. We do all of that under radar, unsanctioned."

"You're not in the National database." Their gazes locked.

112

"No. Is that going to be a problem?" he asked.

She nodded. "Yeah, it is."

He frowned and took her hand. "Why? I don't understand."

Swallowing, Jackie looked away for a few seconds and then met his gaze. "My sire..."

She must have waited too long. "Go on, what about him?"

"He's La Patron."

Quinn stared into her bluish-green eyes and swore he'd misheard his mate. "What?"

"I'm Jackie Knight, daughter of Silas and Jasmine Knight, La Patron and La Patroness." Her voice strengthened at the end.

He stood, releasing her hand and without realizing it, backed away. A myriad of thoughts tumbled through his mind. Chief among them: his mate would be a widower before sunrise if what he heard about the callous hearted Alpha was true. "Your sire? La Patron? Head Alpha?" He needed to be sure.

"Yes. Is that a problem?" She crossed her arms beneath her breasts. For a moment, he simply stared at the towel covered globes, remembering their softness, taste. "Quinn?"

His gaze snapped up and met hers.

"Is it a problem?"

He ran his hand through his hair and shook his head. Since his parents died in an accident, Ramos had been the one stable person in his life. Pack was supposed to be about coming together for the good of everyone else but the only place he ever saw that was with his uncle and Antwan.

Not La Patron or his Alphas or other wolves. Full-bloods attacked and killed his sire. His mam died shortly after. Quinn had no love for most full-bloods and saw them as bullies. He didn't dislike La Patron with the same vitriol Ramos did but he had no respect for the man either. Breeds, like him, who didn't register in the national database were penalized by La Patron's death decree or picked off by the rebels. There was no safe place for those who wanted to live in peace apart from the national pack, which wasn't fair in his book.

Jackie stood and headed for the door.

"Wait." Quinn touched her shoulder.

She shrugged him off and glared at him to hide the pain in her chest. "I don't need this."

"I need you." He waved his hand. "The other stuff we... we'll work out." He wasn't sure how but losing Jackie wasn't an option he could explore.

"I love my parents, my family, Quinn. That's a problem for you, but they aren't going anywhere." Facing him she took a deep breath. "Look, what you and Ramos are doing is important, it needs to be protected. If we... if this mating thing didn't happen I'd be all on board for keeping quiet about it."

Quinn didn't like where this was going. When she remained silent he prompted. "But now, you're going to tell them?" He didn't mean to sound accusatory but his uncle and his uncle's mate worked years, decades helping and saving innocent lives. La Patron wasn't known for his kindness when his orders were disobeyed.

She stiffened and stepped back, dislodging his hand. "Don't talk or think for me. What I was going to say, being mated I can't hide or dismiss you. If we are a couple --"

"We are." That wasn't up for debate. He took her hands in his and waited for her to finish her point.

"As my mate, you'll meet my parents, enter the Compound, and meet my extended family. There are a lot of us. I have two older brothers, Rone and Rese. They're breeds and help run KnightForce and the National database."

"Great." His stomach clenched knowing he would enter the wolf's den and possibly be devoured.

"They are great." She paused, and squeezed his hand. "Take some time, think about it."

"What?" Had he missed something?

"You didn't know, didn't sign up for this... meeting or being a part of La Patron's family."

"Facing criminal charges, entering his den, most importantly...mating with his daughter. No I didn't know but now that I do, I can't walk away from you." He pulled her into his arms and placed a kiss on top of her head. "It's not that I'm a rebel and fight against La Patron specifically." I've heard he was a cold-hearted, arrogant bastard, who destroyed those who disagreed with him and I don't want to be anywhere near him, he thought. "But I broke the law by not registering and that's a punishable offense. I can't bring that to Ramos' door. He's too important." Again, he remembered the stories of La Patron's abuse when he was a young pup and cringed. The bloodshed and killings of those who opposed him were legendary. "How do I protect my uncle from La Patron probing my mind and gaining information? That's what's worrying me. The man took me in and cared for me most of my life, I don't want my good fortune of finding you to be his down-fall." Which was true, just not all the truth.

She rubbed her face against his chest. His palm slid beneath her damp hair. He grabbed a fistful and pulled. Their gazes met for a brief second before he brushed his lips against hers. She shuddered and held him tighter. He took her mouth prisoner, deepening their kiss to banish the thought of her ruthless sire.

When they broke apart, he'd removed her towel, leaving them both naked, skin to delicious skin, in the middle of the room. "I can't give you up," he said against her mouth.

"I don't want you to."

"I need a lifetime with you," he said.

"Sounds like a plan, we'll work out the rest."

Quinn picked her up and carried her into the bedroom. Their clothes were scattered on the floor and the sheets were half off the bed. Releasing her slowly he turned toward the linen closet, and retrieved clean sheets. Together they made quick work of the change but that gave him a moment to think clearer.

"Are you the real reason we're in a safe house and not those rebels from the restaurant?"

She exhaled and he knew the answer. "Yes." She looked across the bed at him. "We've been trained since we came into our wolves to remain human deep when not at the Compound, even on pack lands. I'm not an ambassador for Daddy so he doesn't want pack to approach me on his behalf. It still happens because some recognize me from events with him and Mama. But his scent is strong and a variation of it runs through us."

Glad they were in the basement, Quinn nodded. "But he doesn't know."

"Nionis knows. I'm sure Chip, Nionis' security guy told Alpha Gilbert." She stopped, her hand flew to her mouth as her eyes widened. "Daddy knows," she whispered watching him.

If fear rolled off her at that revelation, Quinn would've grabbed his mate and ran. However, what he sensed was surprise that she hadn't thought of those dots being connected. Neither had he, but he hadn't known about La Patron.

"Yeah, pretty sure he knows by now. He told your sister, right? That's why she's coming?"

Jackie shook her head slowly. "No, I told Renee. By the time she gets here, she'll figure out he already knows." She shook her head with a wry grin. "She's taking the jet. Of course they'll know why she's coming. I didn't think... neither of us was thinking straight. My parents know I'm mated."

"But they haven't said anything?" Quinn tried to get a handle on the Alpha wolf he'd heard horror stories about when he was younger.

"No. Which means he knows you aren't in the database." Concern clouded her gaze.

"He knows the Goddess mated you to a criminal." He tried to lighten the atmosphere.

"Not funny," she snapped. "It's been almost 20 years since the database went national and became a punishable offense in the past five."

"Again," Quinn said watching her closely. "It was a punishable by death offense before La Patron mated. After mating he relaxed the law."

"He didn't know about half-breeds then," she said defensively.

Quinn snorted. "Really? Ramos mother, Arianna, was around for decades. Breeds were everywhere, how could he not know?"

She crossed her arms beneath her breasts and glared at him. "Are you implying he knew about breeds and did nothing about them? Or that he was incompetent in his leadership by not knowing? Which is it?"

"Neither. It's a question. Only he knows the answer."

"Why don't you like him? Have you ever met him?" She sounded genuinely curious, baffled even.

"Not like him? I never said that. I've never met him and don't know him. Plus, no one knows your sire the way you do. He's a very powerful Alpha who's been around a long time. You don't remain in the top position without meeting challenges head-on." He shrugged. "People get hurt."

"Enough generalities," she snapped. "Did he do something to you? Your sire or mam?"

"He killed Arianna. My mam's mam. You would call her my grandmother."

Jackie frowned. "Are you sure? I've never heard of any woman being killed."

Quinn shrugged and kneeled on the bed waiting for her to join him. They could talk just as easily lying down. She crawled toward him. He pulled her close, her head lay on his chest while she pulled the covers over them.

Settled, he inhaled the fresh scent of her damp hair and rubbed his chin across the top. "Yes, I'm sure. Ramos told us, happened a while back." According to Ramos his mam was punch drunk with power she'd acquired over the years and went after La Patron. No one was sure what happened once she arrived at La Patron's compound, but the agonizing screams and curses toward La Patron she sent through her mental link to some of her pups left a chilling mark.

Neither spoke for a few moments. "He won't kill you, but he will question you, ask why you broke the law, things like that. If Ramos knew we were mated he'll understand once you tell him. Find out from him what you can say and can't."

"Ask me questions? Talk to me?" Quinn asked.

"You sound surprised."

"Because he doesn't have to. He can pull my wolf, find out anything he wants without saying shit to me and there's nothing I can do about it." He didn't bother hiding his irritation over being helpless, it had always pissed him off that someone, anyone could level his defenses so easily.

"Go human deep. To break that he'd have to destroy you and he won't do that."

Quinn stilled. Did Jackie realize she'd just chosen him over her sire? "That I can do. What about you? Will he pull information about Ramos from you?"

"No. I've locked it down so no one can access it. But..." She leaned back and looked up at him. "Information on Ramos is all

I've blocked from him. Be prepared to be thoroughly investigated. Come clean about med school, helping kids, staying off the grid to fight the rebels, your parents, all of it. Most importantly, register in the database, today. No more illegal stuff. We've gotta come clean. I prefer you fix this before I tell my parents about us. Since they probably already know, the longer you wait the worse it is. Trust me when I say you don't want him or my mom coming here to check on us because I haven't checked in with them."

Meeting the equivalent of a king, let alone claiming said king's daughter as his mate, made Quinn's stomach clench. Goosebumps flashed across his skin and he fought the dark specter of fear threatening to overtake him. "We can do that now. We passed a computer on the way to the bedroom."

When she rolled out the bed, put on his shirt and headed toward the door in a flash, he realized how serious she was about him giving up his freedom. Thinking over his options, Quinn followed slower. By the time he reached her, she sat at the desk in the office area, clicking keys.

"I've got the main page opened." Jackie stood, stepped to the side and waved him into the chair.

"Pull over that seat." He pointed to an upholstered office chair while looking at the screen. The landing page showed happy, smiling litters of people who appeared healthy, whole and full of promise. Unfortunately, many dual-natureds didn't live or look that way. He paused, thought about what he was about to do. All those years he had avoided detection. Jackie's question, "why didn't he like La Patron" surprised and made him think. He had no personal beef with their leader other than the man had a blind spot when it came to pack members living their lives outside the pack. If he were being honest, he despised La Patron based on what he'd been told. That wasn't right, he needed to investigate the Alpha for himself. Fate stepped in and gave him that chance. He glanced at his mate and touched the keyboard.

Following prompt after prompt, he filled in his information, answered Jackie's questions about his family history and 15 minutes later uploaded photo. "Done." He faced Jackie who appeared relieved.

She leaned forward, wrapped her arms around his neck. "Thank you." She kissed him.

Eager for more, he deepened the kiss. By the time they finished, she was on his lap. "I need to talk to Ramos," Quinn said softly.

Jackie nodded and eased off his lap. "I'll fix us something to eat." She moved to the kitchen area and opened the refrigerator.

"Uncle Ramos." Quinn watched Jackie pull out meat, eggs and cheese.

You've emerged."

Quinn's lips twitched. *Yes, but --"*

Mates are the greatest gifts from the Goddess. Jackie is a brilliant strategist who walks in both worlds with ease, you are blessed by such a beautiful, compassionate wolf."

Who's also La Patron's daughter."

What? That monster! Tell me you are in no way mated to anyone with his blood."

Quinn hadn't expected his uncle's angry response. A part of him assumed Nionis spilled the beans already. Quinn repeated his remark and added he enrolled in the database at his mate's request.

Already? With no warning? You should've told me, given us enough time to move the pups," the older man snapped.

Still reeling with the knowledge of a looming, personal interaction with La Patron, Quinn wasn't in the mood for a scolding. *My mate asked. I complied. You would've done the same thing."* He explained his and Jackie's plan to protect Ramos, the ranch and the children.

I fear that won't be enough but thanks for considering our position."

Quinn thought he heard a sharp twang of sarcasm but wasn't sure. *Her sister is arriving to meet me today."*

Yes, there are four litter mates in addition to two older ones. Good fighters, brutal and inflexible in their allegiance to their ruler."

Ruler? Ramos said things like that about La Patron all the time. Listening to Jackie's love for her sire, Quinn wasn't sure La Patron was the ruthless, immoral, Alpha he had heard about all his life. His mate was too sane, balanced and family oriented for La Patron to be a crazed psychopath.

How're the pups? No need to dwell on what wouldn't be changed. He was now in the half-breed database.

Good, good. Craig still asks about Jackie. I guess he won't see her again. Ramos paused. *What are you going to do? Return here? Pack your things? Stay there? Return with her? What?"*

Quinn hadn't gotten that far. *"You do remember what it's like when you enter the mating heat?"*

Ramos chuckled. *"Fair enough. When your gray mental cells flare to life again, let me know."*

Will do."

"And be careful, your beast is changing. Not only will he not allow another male near your mate, you'll be feral, ready to destroy any perceived threat to your union."

"Perceived?" Quinn couldn't imagine he'd try to destroy anyone based on a hunch. Saving lives was his profession.

"Your beast is in charge of the mating and will prove to his mate he's the best and only person capable of protecting and providing for her. Your human side is just along for the ride and pleasure. I'm just warning you so you won't be surprised or think something's wrong when you behave out of character. Protecting Jackie, making and keeping her happy will drive your actions from now on."

Quinn didn't know what to say. *"Thanks, I appreciate the heads up."* They disconnected. He strode toward the smell of cooked meat and fried potatoes. He stole a slice of bacon and popped it into his mouth before Jackie could stop him.

Smiling, she split the meat, eggs and potatoes onto plates, giving him the larger portions. They ate in silence. When they finished, he took her plate along with his and washed them.

"Everything okay?" Jackie sat sipping juice at the table.

"Yeah. He was concerned that he'd need to move the children." Quinn looked over his shoulder at her.

"I was thinking about that," she said slowly. "What if we got the ranch sanctioned to do what it's doing? Chances are Alpha Gilbert already knows and allows it."

"No." Ramos' dislike of La Patron went beyond the ranch.

"No? Why not? We could help more pups."

"It works the way it is, leave it alone." He didn't want to argue or explain Ramos' personal beef with her father.

"Not really. Ramos could do more if he wasn't in the shadows."

"The shadows help others trust him." When the confused look on her face remained, he tried a different approach. "We aren't the only ones who don't trust the database. Lots of breeds aren't registered. You think they'd trust Ramos if he was on La Patron's radar?"

Frowning, she put down her fork and stared at him. "Trust? Radar? What aren't you telling me?"

Seriously? She still thought the world was bright and cheery after seeing Craig, Sean and the girls. They were the lucky ones who escaped. "Not everyone is a rebel who doesn't enroll in the database."

"Who break the law," she stressed watching him closely.

He clamped his jaw and released it slowly. "Right, it's illegal not to enroll, but the reasons for not doing it aren't the same as rebels who hate breeds, at least that's the lie they peddle to recruit. But it doesn't matter to ... those in charge. We're all painted with the same brush, called rebels if we don't comply, when that's not true."

"Different levels, different kinds of rebellion?" she asked a few seconds later.

He thought about it. "Maybe, but not the malicious intent. I didn't enroll in the database because I wanted to continue helping save the pups. I've had pups whose parents didn't want to be on pack lands or had been shunned for one thing or another. Maybe they didn't see the benefits offered in the national pack, or were accustomed to living apart in small groups and didn't bother. But reasons don't matter. If you don't do it, you're a rebel, law-breaker, end of story. When that's not the end, it's a different story that hasn't been told."

They stared at each other for a few moments. "How many do you think haven't registered?"

Quinn shook his head. "Have no idea. But it's not unusual. Before breeds were accepted, Alphas always had remnants of those who lived on the fringes, away from pack lands, doing their own thing within their smaller packs."

"You blame my... La Patron for being too harsh? Not understanding?"

"I blame no one. We're having a conversation. You asked. I answered." Finished with the dishes and the conversation, he extended his hand to her. "Sex?"

She glared at him a few moments before standing and taking his hand. "Yes, please."

He smiled. "So polite, I like that."

She grabbed his cock. "I like this."

CHAPTER SIXTEEN

Several hours later, alert to added security driving behind them, Jackie and Quinn pulled into Nionis' driveway. Renee walked out the door and stood on the porch watching. Wearing snug pair of designer jeans and cream tee with five-inch ankle boots, Renee's sleek hair lay in perfect dark waves across her shoulders and back. Regardless how casual she dressed Renee always looked polished and runway perfect.

Happiness spiraled inside Jackie's chest as she twirled one of her unruly curls. Exiting the car, they held hands as they strolled forward. Seeing her sister's smile Jackie released Quinn's hand and extended her arms toward Renee.

The two embraced. It felt good.

Handsome," Renee said through their link.

You think?" Jackie teased as they pulled apart.

Yeah, he looks nerdy and sexy, an interesting combination. What does he do?"

Doctor. "Jackie glanced at Quinn who hadn't moved and continued to watch them. She hadn't thought of him as nerdy.

Surprising. He seems a cross between David and Adam, studious yet adventurous."

Jackie looked at her sister with a narrowing gaze. Had Renee researched Quinn? Granted, as an artist Renee saw things from a different perspective, allowing her to capture the essence of whatever she choose to paint or draw, but Jackie hadn't realized that talent extended to people.

You pegged him without him saying a word. Did you research him? Jackie asked.

No. But you can look at him and tell he's no pushover. The way he's watching patiently while we greet each other says a lot about him as well. He's alert, probably could tell you where every person is standing within 50 feet of you. But he also has that look of an academic, like you. Renee smiled, looped her arm in Jackie's and took a step toward Quinn. "Hello, I'm Renee."

Jackie groaned. "Quinn, this is my litter mate, the one we specifically drove over here to meet you."

Quinn smiled but didn't move. "Hi Renee, welcome to Tennessee."

Without releasing Renee, Jackie extended her hand, he took it and they entered the double doors of Nionis' home. Inside Nionis stood in the living room with a welcoming smile. Heavenly aromas of cooked meats and other foodstuffs filled the air causing Jackie's stomach to growl.

Quinn grinned.

"Glad you made it," Nionis said offering Jackie a wide smile. "Food's done."

"We promise not to mention you being over an hour late," Renee said releasing Jackie and heading toward the kitchen.

Heat flew to Jackie's face. She glanced at Quinn, noticed he took the comment in stride and relaxed. Renee spoke her mind and some people didn't appreciate her off-beat brand of humor. But Renee had a heart of gold once you got past her defenses.

"Thanks, I appreciate that," Jackie said heading toward the dining area. Platters of baked chicken, ribs and steaks sat in the middle of the table. Steaming side dishes of mac and cheese, yams, greens, beans and peas lined the side buffet table. Jackie handed Quinn a plate and looked at the cakes and pastries on the buffet behind them.

Quinn filled the plate with a little of everything and handed it back to her. Surprised, Jackie blinked a couple times before accepting it.

"What do you want to drink?" he asked staring into her eyes.

"Water. A bottle of water." She held up the plate of food. "Thanks."

He leaned in and brushed his lips against hers. When his mouth touched hers, Jackie forgot where they were, who was in the room and that she held a full plate of food in her hand. The kiss, getting closer to him, tasting more, occupied her mind. With her free hand, she grabbed a fistful of his shirt, pulled and opened her mouth. He removed the plate, and pulled her close, deepening their kiss. Once again, heat erupted between them. Her fingertips inched into his hair. His strong hands clasped her ass, lifting her against his hardness. She ached to be filled by him and wrapped her legs around his waist.

Jackie, you need to stop," Renee said through their link.

They broke apart on a gasp. Jackie rested her forehead against his and bit her bottom lip. A chair scraped the floor. Sounds of eating and drinking filtered through her lust-filled mind. Leaning back, she met Quinn's smoldering gaze and swallowed hard.

"Hungry?" Jackie asked him in a low, lusty growl.

"Eating here," Renee said from the other side of the room.

Quinn released her slowly down his front while leaving their next move up to her. She took a deep breath and looked at her plate on the table.

Renee snickered as Jackie pulled out the chair in front of her and plopped onto the upholstered cushion. Quinn placed a bottle of water next to her.

"Thanks," Jackie whispered meeting Renee's amused gaze.

Quinn squeezed her shoulder and left to fix his plate.

Girl, Nionis said. "*He must've worked you over because you've been walking crooked since you got out the car.*"

Jackie's face heated but she didn't respond to the teasing. "This tastes good." She held up a fork full of food and ate.

"Hungry?" Renee asked smiling from the other side of the table.

"Famished," Jackie said without missing a beat.

"I'm sure you are," Nionis said as Quinn returned to the table, sitting next to Jackie.

He glanced at Jackie. "Need anything?"

More heat raced to her face as she read the promise in his eyes.

"He's talking about the food, Jackie," Renee said.

"I know that," Jackie said grinning. "No thanks, I'm good."

Quinn ate his first plate in silence.

Jackie lingered on hers a bit, thinking of their time together at the safe house. She still hadn't contacted her parents but planned to do so soon. Maybe she'd put Quinn on the phone, let them talk a bit. The idea had merit. Mama wouldn't grill him but her dad... she wasn't sure what he'd say or ask. Maybe she'd just wait.

Quinn speared a piece of steak she'd cut from her plate and ate it drawing her attention.

"Have you always lived in Tennessee?" Renee asked Quinn.

"No. I moved in with my uncle after my parents died."

"I'm sorry about your parents," Renee said.

Quinn nodded and continued eating.

"Welcome to the family," Renee said.

Quinn's brow rose. "Thank you."

I like him for you," Renee told Jackie.

Really? Why?" Curious, Jackie looked across the table and met her sister's blue gaze.

He fixed your plate first, made sure you had what you needed before seeing to his own needs. Most importantly I don't think he sees anyone else in this room." Renee took a sip of water from her glass. "*The two of you threw off so much heat during that kiss, I thought the walls would catch fire.*"

I can't help responding to him," Jackie said as Quinn stiffened next to her and stood. She hated they weren't able to mind link yet, according to Ramos it happened sometime during their bonding. She grabbed Quinn's hand and looked up at him.

"Ramos and the pups were attacked."

Nionis gasped.

Jackie's chest hurt as she stood and moved closer to Quinn. "Where? When? What happened?"

Quinn glanced at Renee, took Jackie's hand and headed to the front exit. "I've got to go help them."

"What happened?" Jackie asked again as they strode to his vehicle.

They sat in the car and he turned it on. "He wanted the pups moved from the ranch." Quinn met her gaze. "He doesn't trust La Patron and with our connection..." Quinn shook his head and she read the guilt in them. "Rebels attacked the van on the road. I've got to help track them."

Cold dread slid down Jackie's spine. "Did they take the pups?"

Quinn nodded. "Ramos thinks they plan to kill Marsha."

Jackie gasped. Unable to speak past the lump of fear in her throat, she shook her head.

"I'll be back after... later, but I need to head out." He leaned forward and brushed a kiss against her mouth.

She understood he needed to go, but fear lodged protests in her throat. "Be careful."

His large palm cupped her cheek. "I will. Go, visit with your sister. Stay here with security. I'll contact you when I know more."

Jackie kissed the inside of his hand and slid out of the car tamping down words to make him stay. Her beast whined as he pulled out the drive and down the street. Slowly, she returned to the house to face her sister's questions. The rebels forced her hand, now she'd need to share Ramos' secret and develop a plan to help save the pups.

CHAPTER SEVENTEEN

Rebels? Are you crazy?" Renee asked as Jackie changed into black jeans, tee and hiking boots.

Not crazy. Motivated to do something." Jackie glanced at her watch and wished Nionis would hurry. They needed to move now.

But... you're going hunting for people KnightForce can't find," Renee said standing in front of her sister to slow her down. *"Call them, let them do their jobs. You shouldn't be running behind Quinn into danger. Does he have experience?"*

Jackie regretted sharing the little information about Ramos and Quinn with her sister. Renee had been wailing her doubts since Jackie and Nionis decided to join the hunt. First, Nionis had to secure Chip's promise to keep their efforts a secret just as Renee had.

We need to move out," Jackie told Nionis who was downstairs pleading her cause with Chip.

Almost there. Can you calm down Renee? If I feel her distress, others may as well."

Jackie spun to face Renee and pointed. *Look, I shared something really important to me. I love those pups and if Marsha or any of them die while I hide behind Daddy's shield, or do nothing I'll never forgive myself. So stop bitching."*

128

Telling KnightForce is doing something," Renee snapped undeterred.

"*You said it yourself, KnightForce can't find them. If they've never found the rebels before, they won't find them now. I won't risk the pups that way.* 'She picked up her small pack of blades and placed it in her pocket while wondering if she should take a gun. Her parents made sure they could all defend themselves against all threats, human and dual-natureds.

You're really going all vigilante?" Renee said into the silence. Jackie snorted. *Leave it to you to call it that.*"

Feels like I'm seeing a different part of you, that's all. If anyone had asked if you'd do this." Renee waved at Jackie. *I would've said no.*"

Jackie thought about it for a few seconds. *You may be right. Things happen in life that opens our eyes to situations we had no idea existed. Once we learn about them we can't ignore what we've seen or know is true.* 'She paused. "*I held that little boy, talked to Marsha and laid on a bed with Penny. They aren't faceless pups to me. Listening to their stories, learning their hardships, their lives so different from mine and others... it changed me. Changed what I want to do with my life.*"

What's that?"

Make a difference for those who join the pack and those who don't.

What do you mean those who don't? That's illegal. 'Renee crossed her arms and returned Jackie's stare.

Jackie shrugged. What Quinn said made sense. *Some create smaller packs and it fits them better. They're still dual-natured wolves and not necessarily rebels.*"

Don't get it twisted, they are rebels if they don't join the pack," Renee said in a hard tone. *The stuff about the pups, I get that but the rest of it... no. That's wrong. We have pack for a reason. Safety, security, sharing of resources, and others. That's what makes the rebels so dangerous. They stop pack members from getting the help they need.*"

Jackie didn't bother arguing points she knew better than Quinn's name. Instead she shrugged and headed for the door. Downstairs, Nionis, dressed similarly to Jackie, nodded.

Let's go. I've got an area mapped on my phone where they may be hiding, we'll start there," Jackie told Nionis.

Have you told Quinn we're coming?" Nionis asked.

No. His phone went to voice mail. When we are on the move you can tell Ramos, not before. 'She pinned Nionis with a look to show how serious she was about this.

Nionis nodded.

Jackie headed toward the garage, mentally calculating scenarios, tactics and probabilities at lightning speed. There was a good chance they'd find the pups, but would it be in time to save Marsha and Penny? The two females were in the most danger.

Chip's in the truck out front, 'Nionis said behind her.

As much as she would've preferred to do this on their own, ditching security with two La Patron pups in the state was a pipe dream. Jackie altered directions mid-stride and headed toward the door.

"Wait," Renee yelled from the staircase behind them.

Jackie didn't stop. Outside she slid in the back seat and pulled out her phone. Nionis sat upfront with Chip. Renee slid in next to Jackie.

What are you doing? 'Jackie asked unable to hide her surprise at seeing her fashionable litter-mate in baggy black jeans and over-sized black Tee. She didn't think Renee owned a tee-shirt or black steel toe boots.

Renee closed the door and waved for Jackie to move over so she'd have more room. The SUV pulled out the driveway. *I'm going with you. Maybe I need to see what you've seen instead of repeating what I learned in school. Obviously, I'm missing something. 'She* shrugged and patted her thick ponytail. *"This is important to you and you believe it needs to be done. That's enough for me."*

Jackie started to remind her sister of her recent opposition but stopped. *"Thanks, this is important. Everything's not black or white. Pups are being abused and that's not right."*

Then we help them by shining light on a gray area so others can't take advantage of them. 'Renee paused. *Is there time to get a decent pair of hiking boots?"*

No." Jackie continued looking at her phone and instructed Nionis to tell Chip where to drive.

Being mated changed you," Renee said.

Startled, Jackie looked across the seat at her. *Really?"*

Renee nodded. *"This whole search the mountains, break laws if necessary, save the world dressed in black, which looks really good on you by the way, is new"*

I'd like to think I'd have changed if I saw the pups anyway." Jackie shrugged off the compliment, sat back and looked out the window. Was Renee right? Jackie didn't think so but if Quinn was the catalyst for her helping the pups she could live with that just fine.

Probably. Listen I know I agreed to keep this between the two of us and I will. Renee held up her hand to stop Jackie's protest. *But when we're done, we'll need to share what we learned with everybody. If your gray area prediction is right, Mama and Daddy need to know so they can fix it. It's not fair to keep this kind of information away from them."*

Jackie didn't say anything. She had planned to talk to her parents about Quinn today after the meal, but things derailed after the Ramos' message. Still, Renee was right, eventually they'd need to come clean about a lot of things. Jackie inhaled.

Good thing eventually wasn't right now.

Twenty minutes later they drove on US 441S through the mountains. Jackie re-read the information Ramos sent Nionis regarding the attack. Renee sat quietly on the other side looking out the window. Nionis laughed aloud periodically, probably from a mind-link conversation with someone, otherwise silence filled the air. None of them were prepared when the rear window shattered and smoke filled the car.

"Quinn!" Jackie yelled as thick smoke filled her nostrils and the vehicle swerved across the road and finally stopped.

"Jackie. I can hear you," Quinn said through a mental link.

She didn't respond to the surprise in his voice. *"Smoke. Car. Help."* A cool wind blew down the link clearing her mind. Renee and Nionis lay slumped in their seats. Chip managed to turn off the truck but now lay slumped over the steering wheel unmoving.

Jackie pushed some of the cool wind to Renee. *"Wake up and fight this,"* she told her sister as a sense of foreboding rolled over her. Someone was coming.

"What?" Renee moaned.

Quiet someone's coming, I need to wake Nionis. Hoping her litter mate could fight back on her own, Jackie reached out to Nionis.

I'm good, Nionis surprised her. *Ramos cleared the way for me while Quinn took care of you. I think we should see where this leads."*

What? Jackie wondered if Nionis had lost her mind.

Hear me out, Nionis said. *"These are the ones we're tracking. This is how they got Ramos and the pups off the road, right?"*

Yeah. Jackie hadn't thought about that.

They may take us to the pups. Ramos is locked onto me, Quinn to you. They're already on their way, why not lead them to the pups?"

Something could go wrong and my sister could get hurt," Jackie said, already feeling guilty about Renee being a part of this.

"Let her stay here or have her escape and go home," Nionis said.

"Get real, Renee would never leave me like that," Jackie said feeling trapped. Nionis' idea was good on several levels. At the very least she could talk to her father in case things got out of hand. He had shown them how he could intervene on their behalf no matter where they were in the world.

True. Someone's here, just watching for now. Maybe waiting to see if anyone stops to help," Nionis said.

Or waiting for backup. They need a vehicle to move us if they don't take this one, Jackie said looking at Renee and sending more fresh air down their link.

I think we should wait, let them take us and then rescue the pups, Nionis said.

Other than Renee getting hurt, Jackie couldn't think of another reason not to follow through. All three of them had trained with KnightForce agents from time to time and were just as lethal. Additionally, she and Renee could use David and Adam's energies and abilities if necessary to defeat an enemy. They'd practiced that type of fighting over and over until her father was comfortable with their skills.

Okay. I hope they hurry, I can't stop worrying about Marsha and Penny, Jackie said.

132

Me neither, 'Nionis agreed.

Moments later a van pulled up behind them with a medical emblem on the side. Four men in white coats approached the SUV while the first person on the scene remained at a distance. The doors opened, three of them were lifted from their seats and taken to the van.

If they plan to hurt Chip, we stop this now," Jackie told Nionis.

These four won't hurt him, I don't know about the one watching. Security is almost here, they'll get Chip. 'Nionis paused. *Now would be a good time to tell your parents you're okay because security will call it in that we're missing."*

Jackie thought over it for a bit. Since she could link with her father she swallowed her pride and reached out.

Jackie? How's Tennessee? 'her dad asked.

Hearing the deep cadence of his voice made her feel like a little girl with her arms stretched for him to pick her up and make everything alright. Eyes closed, she tightened the lid on Ramos and the ranch. *"Hi Daddy, I've got something to tell you and Mama."*

CHAPTER EIGHTEEN

*Jackie....Jackie!'*Quinn continued yelling through the tenuous link he'd held a few moments with his mate. Eyes widening as realization dawned. *"She's not responding,* 'he told his uncle. *"Why can't I reach her? Mates are supposed to be connected. What's happening?"*

Ramos placed his hand on Quinn's shoulder as Antwan pressed the gas pedal in the jeep. "It's a new connection. Sometimes they're unstable, especially in stressful situations. I've got a link on Nionis and your mate's fine. The rebels took the women but left their security guard. Nionis sensed another full-blood near their truck."

Quinn's gut tightened at the idea of his mate in the hands of his enemies. *Jackie,* 'he called through their link again.

"She thinks it's the wolf who shot the gas canister in their truck... and ours," Ramos said.

Quinn growled low in his throat.

"If he's still there when we get close, he's mine," Antwan said in a low menacing tone.

"We have to catch up with the rebels," Quinn said, eager to make sure Jackie was okay.

"Won't take long," Antwan said as their vehicle shot down the highway. A few moments later, they slowed. "I see their SUV on the side of the road. One heartbeat in the truck, another creeping forward." He glanced at Ramos and unbuckled his seat-belt. "Take the wheel."

Knowing it was useless to argue, Quinn searched for signs of his mate or her state of mind when she was taken. One second Antwan was in the driver seat, the next he jumped out the jeep. The vehicle swerved, straightened as his uncle took the wheel until it slowed to a stop on the side of the road.

Quinn and his uncle jumped out and ran across the street. The full-blood who'd been creeping toward the SUV took off into the woods.

Antwan and Quinn followed.

As soon as they entered the tree line both shifted and took off after the full-blood. With the scent of his prey in his nostrils, a new level of anger roared through Quinn unleashing a feral side of his beast. *Death to the one who harmed his mate.*

Death. Death. Death. The word rolled through his mind with singular purpose. He caught sight of the rebel jumping a fallen log and stumble. Eager to capitalize on the rebel's misfortune, Quinn quickened his stride, jumping from boulder to boulder until he saw the rebel on the ground beneath him standing slowly, preparing to run. Quinn leapt, landed on the rebel's back, knocking him down.

Antwan reached them just as Quinn made contact. "*Mine,*" Antwan said through their link.

We need information, 'Quinn said hoping Antwan would listen. But if this wolf had anything to do with taking the pups from Ramos, he would die painfully at Antwan's hands.

Rather than respond, Antwan grabbed the downed beast by the neck, and growled so low the vibration went through ground. He dropped the beast and it shifted. Antwan shifted, picked up the full-blood by the neck and shook him.

Quinn didn't want the rebel killed until they learned where Jackie had been taken.

The full-blood tried to break Antwan's grip but couldn't. Quinn morphed to human. "*We don't have time to string this out.*" His body shook with need to be closer to his mate.

He won't talk," Antwan said.

Kill him and let's go. 'Out of patience and fearing his beast would take control and seek their mate, Quinn turned to head back to the jeep.

Antwan threw the rebel on the ground at Quinn's feet. *He set up your mate to be taken."*

A low growl erupted from Quinn as his beast took control. Spinning, he grabbed the full blood by the hair, lifting him from the ground and slammed his fist into his face repeatedly, breaking bones. Fueled by the thought of his mate in danger because of this asshole, Quinn stepped outside his medical training, his commitment to save life and used every bit of knowledge he possessed to damage the full-blood in ways he would never recover from.

"Pleeeeease," the full-blood begged as Quinn dug into a pressure point near his jawline.

"Why did you attack us today?" Antwan asked, placing his hand on Quinn's shoulder.

Quinn's body shuddered with effort to pull back the murderous rage enveloping him.

"Stop," the rebel panted.

Swallowing hard, Quinn eased up but didn't release him. His beast growled and snapped against his human side for control.

"Answer me," Antwan said stooping close to them on the ground.

"Pups," he whispered.

"You had the pups and attacked the second truck," Antwan said squeezing Quinn's shoulder to stop him from doing more damage.

"The pup wanted her... told us about the others."

"What are your plans for the others?" Antwan asked watching Quinn who took short sips of air to contain his beast.

"Don't know."

Antwan grabbed the full-blood by the back of his head and lifted it to face him. The rebel grimaced from being in such an odd angle but Antwan gave no respite. "Lie again and he'll break you." Antwan tipped his head at Quinn who fought his beast to remain in human form.

"Breeding," the rebel whispered and screamed.

136

The moment the word was uttered Quinn lost the battle with his beast and shifted. Antwan flung the full blood to the ground. Quinn jumped on him and bit down on his back, crushing bones. The rebel shifted and tried to fight but it was too late, Quinn fought through a haze of hatred and vengeance. This beast had taken his mate, placed her in harm's way to be touched by others and would die for that by his hand.

Quinn broke the full-blood's neck. In death, it returned to its human form. Antwan picked up the rebel and tossed him into the forest. Quinn shifted and headed back to the jeep, Antwan followed in silence. They broke through the trees and saw Ramos and two other shifters. Eager to find Jackie, Quinn strode to the jeep while Antwan headed to his mate.

Jackie... Jackie, 'Quinn sat in the back seat with his arms wrapped around his waist rocking as he called to his mate. His skin grew cold, then hot as he tried to find her. Looking over his shoulder, he growled over the delay in reaching his mate. Canine teeth crowded his mouth as his fingertips turned to claws. Need for his mate gripped his gut, slashing against him. Unable to remain still, holding on to his humanity by a thread, he stepped out the jeep and ran in the direction they'd been going.

He searched for her scent, it was too faint to follow but he'd try even if he had to shift and track her from the woods. Eventually the jeep pulled alongside him. Ramos waved for him to get in. Quinn jumped in the back seat and they took off down the road.

"Alpha Gilbert sent KnightForce and extra security to squash the rebels. They've agreed to allow us to go in to get the pups," Ramos said. "I don't like it or trust them but we have no choice. Either work with them or be left out." He paused. "I think La Patron is involved."

Quinn stared out the window in silence. His mate had been captured, taken from him. Why had she left pack lands where she was safe? Did the pups mean that much to her? He thought about it for a moment. Yes. She would risk her safety to save others.

Antwan turned off the highway onto a dirt path and stopped. "Let's go," Ramos said stepping out and shifting. Within seconds they were deep in the forest. Scenting others nearby, they stopped. Ahead, six full-bloods dressed in camo gear stood in front of a copse of trees, blending nicely

Just as Quinn prepared to rush them, two other full-bloods dressed in black approached from the woods and attacked the six.

"*KnightForce,*" Ramos said. They watched the two agents take on the rebels, moments later the rebels lay prostrate on the ground. One KnightForce agent nodded in their direction and then placed cuffs on the rebels.

"*This way,*" Ramos said. They jogged toward the copse of trees and through them.

Small huts nestled beneath tall pine trees made them invisible from above. No one opened their doors or stopped Quinn's party as they strode toward the parked van in the middle of the path. In the distance a shaft of sunlight broke through the trees, shining on a small vegetable garden.

Did you know these houses were here?" Quinn asked his uncle while searching for Jackie's scent.

I've heard rebels had small towns hidden in the mountains but this is my first time seeing one."Ramos started running. He passed the van and left the small huts behind. Climbing through the mountainous vegetation, he continued until they reached a small clearing. Below, a stone house sat beneath large branches which hid the building from above.

Once the rebel's van started moving Jackie exhaled. So far they'd pulled it off without anyone getting hurt. She prayed the pups were safe wherever the van was headed. She shook with the need to contact her mate. No one ever mentioned this hollow feeling growing inside the longer they were apart or the escalating sense of loss and anxiety gripping her. The positive effect from their mental link grew distant with each passing minute.

Are you okay, Renee?"Jackie peeked beneath her eyelids to see her sister. Renee lay in next to Nionis across from Jackie.

Will you and Daddy stop asking me that? I was trained just like you and the boys how to defend myself. Just because I'm an artist--"

Sorry," Jackie cut her off before the conversation dived into a discussion of the merits of art over other disciplines. Renee was never too tired to talk art. Considering their father planned to merge with Renee and deal with the rebels through her, his asking about her mental and physical condition was critical. If Renee wasn't up to par, when their father linked to her and took over her vision, it could harm Renee.

"Nee, you okay?" Jackie asked Nionis.

"Yeah, uncomfortable in this position but basically good." She paused. *"I haven't told Daddy what's going on yet."*

"What? You told me to tell my dad," Jackie said trying to remain still as if she were still impacted by the smoke bomb.

Nionis gasped. *"You told him?"*

"Yeah. He's not happy and will probably have more to say later but for now he's standing by."

"Standing by?" Nionis sounded confused.

"To help catch the rebels and hopefully find out who's leading them in this area."

"Oh, so he thought it was a good idea to play along as bait?"

Jackie snorted at the hopeful sound in Nionis' voice. *"No. He hated it and had a few words to say about it but in the end understood why we're doing it."* It had helped when she reminded him of KnightForce's failure to get as far as she and Nionis had in a much shorter period of time. He grunted instead of agreeing with her but she'd take that as consent. One thing she knew with absolute certainty, the three of them weren't alone. Her father intended to ride Renee's beast to see the rebels and handle them personally. This would be the last kidnapping any of them would ever do. He agreed to wait until she and Nionis rescued the pups before terminating the rebels.

"That's good I guess. I haven't heard from my dad yet..."

"I'm sure Daddy told him what's going on," Jackie said with confidence. Neither of their parents saw them as full grown pups and would continue to watch over them as if they were still in the den.

"Don't talk around me," Renee complained. *"Let me hear what you guys are talking about."*

Jackie opened their link and brought Renee current on their conversation.

"How'd he take the news of your mating?" Nionis asked.

Renee chuckled.

Jackie bit back a groan. "*Okay I guess. He already knew and asked why'd I taken so long to tell him and Mama.*"

Wow. What did you tell him?" Nionis asked.

Yeah, what'd you tell him?" Renee asked.

Jackie's skin tightened as her face warmed. "*Reminded him of the mating heat,*" she said softly.

Renee's squeal raced down the link but not in the van, something she'd mastered since they were children. *Goddess I wish I could've seen Daddy's face when you said that. Pray he doesn't kill Quinn for making you walk crooked.*"

I don't walk crooked," Jackie snapped, aggravated with the restrictions of lying still and defending herself.

You were," Nionis said.

Yeah, I noticed that familiar stroll, Mama, Danielle, and Rose all walk like that sometimes," Renee said.

And you," Nionis told Renee. "*That's how we all knew when you and Tomas were having sex.*"

Renee's sigh was just as irritating as her squeal. "*Yeah, Tomas is something else. He's got mad skills.*"

Jackie didn't bother responding. Renee and Tomas had something special even if they weren't mates, Jackie knew Renee cared deeply for him.

Someone's coming," Nionis said.

It's not Quinn," Jackie said, disappointed her mate hadn't arrived yet. Her beast had been manageable during the drive but now wanted their mate.

"*No. But they're on their way. Chip's okay, for some reason the chemicals damaged his lungs, he's been taken to the clinic. Alpha Gilbert's upset. KnightForce is involved,*" Nionis told them.

"*Good,*" Renee said. "*They should've been here by now.*"

We had a lead on them," Nionis reminded her.

The door opened. Jackie was lifted and removed from the van. Cool air brushed against her fevered skin as she was taken a few steps forward. Footsteps echoed on wood, the door opened and warm, stale air assaulted her nostrils just as the pups, Craig and Sean, scents reached her. Inhaling, she searched for Penny and Marsha and found those as well.

The pups are here," Jackie told the others.

Let's get them and get out of here," Renee said.

"*Good idea. Renee, tell Daddy we're inside, he'll tell you what to do,*" Jackie said.

"*Okay.*"

"*Nionis, do not allow them to cuff or gas us. Daddy will keep me and Renee clear of the gas, and I'll help you if Ramos can't,*" Jackie said while being placed on a hard surface. She opened her eyes and rolled to the right before the shackles could be placed on her legs.

"Hey, get back up here." A large beefy hand reached for her. She backed away and looked around. Two other full bloods tried to recapture Nionis and Renee. One second the big men were lunging at them, the next they lay whimpering on the ground writhing in pain.

"*Ask Daddy if you need to stay here with these three or can you walk through the house with us?*" Jackie told Renee.

"*He said to go with you, he wants to see everything,*" Renee said as the wolves stopped moving. Jackie left the room and peeked into the hall. Although she smelled the pups, she wasn't sure how to reach them. They left the room and slowly searched all the rooms on that level.

Nothing.

Jackie remembered the safe house and its basement. *Touch the walls, look for a lever or something to open a door leading downstairs,* she told them. They spread out. Nionis went to the kitchen. Renee the bedroom. Jackie re-entered the room they'd been taken.

Stepping over the dead wolves, she spread her palms over the walls, pushing, tapping and searching for a way to the pups. Nothing. Frustrated, she looked around the room one last time before leaving. The table with the cuffs sat in the middle. Where were they going to put Renee and Nionis? Jackie wondered? Why bring them in here with no place to secure them?

She strode to the table and looked beneath it. There were two buttons attached to the side. She pushed one. A series of clicks sounded and the wall moved.

"*I found it,*" she told the others and moved slowly toward the opening.

Renee and Nionis came up behind her.

"*Daddy said for me to go first,*" Renee said moving forward.

Jackie and Nionis stood aside as Renee walked through the entrance down the steps.

Sean, Marsha and the others are down here, 'Nionis said in a pleased tone. The door slid shut behind them. *Shit,* 'Nionis muttered. *I lost Ramos."*

"What?" Jackie said, shutting Renee out of this conversation. Her sister glanced back at her and nodded she understood.

I don't think it's because of where we are, we just hit a bump. He should be back soon."

Is Daddy still with you?" Jackie asked Renee.

Oh yeah, and he's pissed. Mama's keeping him calm but she's upset this is happening too, 'Renee said and then stopped.

Six people behind that door, 'Jackie said. *Not all are our pups."*

Let me try and get a read on them, 'Nionis said closing her eyes. For a few seconds, no one spoke. *"One caregiver, the rest pups.* 'She looked at Jackie. *"Marsha's in bad shape. They beat her, Penny's sitting with her but she's bleeding. We need Quinn here now."*

Daddy can help her, 'Jackie said moving closer to the door, examining the locks and security system. It looked familiar. *We have this system at my job."* She placed her hand above the palm scanner, felt the familiar heat and jerked it back. *"Any ideas on how to get through this door?"*

Try the handle, see if it's locked, 'Nionis said and then shrugged. *Always rule out the easiest probabilities first."*

Renee strode to the door, and turned the handle hard. It opened. She looked at Jackie with a raised brow and tilted head. *Didn't expect that."*

Me neither, 'Jackie said listening to the chatter of the pups. She hadn't expected to hear them talking and laughing. Renee stepped inside and strode down the empty hall until she came to a door. Opening it, she looked inside. The chatter stopped for a few seconds and started again. Nionis and Jackie continued forward searching for Marsha and Penny. After opening two more doors, they finally found the girls in the last room. Marsha lay cuffed and bleeding to a table similar to the one upstairs. Penny was cuffed to a chair next to the bed. Fear filled her eyes when they entered.

142

"What?... Help Marsha. I'm scared she's dying. They... help her please." She pointed to the young woman on the table who bled from numerous cuts and bruises.

Renee, Jackie called. "*We need Daddy's help in here.* 'She looked at Nionis who stood next to Penny. "*Go watch the children so they aren't scared. Help will be here soon.*"

Penny wiped tears from her cheeks as she continued watching Marsha. "She wouldn't let them hurt me, so they beat her," she whispered.

Nionis left and a few seconds later Renee entered and strode to the foot of the bed. She grabbed the metal cuff on Marsha's ankle and pulled it apart. Jackie pulled the cuff apart from her arm and rubbed it gently.

"Step back," Renee said, glancing at Jackie.

Seeing her father's piercing gaze in Renee's eyes, Jackie moved. The next second Marsha lay on the table as a wolf. Renee placed her hands on the beast and closed her eyes. Jackie sensed her father work on healing the young wolf and sent a prayer for Marsha's recovery. When Renee stepped back, Jackie went to her and placed her arm around her sister.

You okay?" she asked searching Renee's eyes to make sure she was fine.

Yeah. It takes a bit out of you even if the energy's not yours. Daddy's catching his breath right now. Mom's on standby. Release her from the chair, she looks uncomfortable. 'Renee waved at Penny who stared at Marsha.

With another look at her sister, Jackie moved quickly to Penny and snapped the cuff holding her to the chair.

"Thanks," Penny said. "Is she going to be alright?" She glanced at Jackie and then back at Marsha's still form.

"In time," Renee said and walked out the room.

Jackie rubbed Marsha's head a few times and was rewarded when the pup licked her palm. Penny stood and started stroking Marsha as well. The door opened. Craig ran to Jackie and threw his short arms around her leg.

"You came for me." He rubbed his face against her leg.

"Of course, I was afraid something happened to you," Jackie said her heart full at seeing the small pup. He raised his arms and she lifted him. Laughter bubbled from her throat as he placed kisses on her face and laid his head on her chest. She looked toward the door and saw Renee, but it was her father's eyes watching.

How are the other children?' Jackie asked.

"They're settling, Nionis is speaking with them getting the story about the kidnapping. The caretaker isn't a rebel per se, she cooks and cares for the pups, like a day-care,' Renee said. *Of course, she doesn't think she's done anything wrong by not reporting this to Alpha Gilbert. It was a job, one that paid well and she enjoyed caring for the pups. She's more concerned about the pups' future than her own."*

Jackie didn't know what to say about that and left it alone. *"Quinn's here."*

Renee turned, looked down the hall and back at her. *"Is he?"*

Jackie's heart raced. Craig lifted his head and looked at her. "What's wrong?"

"Quinn's here." Smiling she looked into the pup's face and back at Marsha who remained on the table.

Craig's face scrunched. "Quinn? The big one?"

Technically Antwan was the biggest but she considered her mate big as well. She nodded. "Yes, he's my mate." Hearing the words uttered from her mouth filled her with excitement and expectation. Giddy with pleasure she twirled the pup around in her arms while laughing for no particular reason other than sheer happiness.

The door to the basement opened. Renee stepped aside and leaned against the wall watching.

"Jackie?" Quinn's voice filled the air and his footsteps followed. Seconds later he raced into the room, picked her up and while holding both her and Craig, kissed her. She wrapped one arm around his shoulder holding him close, enjoying the pleasure of his touch and scent.

"Are you okay? We saw the bodies upstairs..." he asked stepping back giving her a quick visual examination before pulling her close again.

"Yes. I'm fine. Marsha's not." She met his gaze and then looked at the pup on the table.

"You got her to shift?" Holding her hand, he stepped toward the table and placed his hand on Marsha who raised her head to look at him and then lay it back down.

"No. Daddy pulled her wolf." She prayed he wouldn't say anything out of line.

"Good, that's the best thing for her." He kissed the back of Jackie's hand before releasing it and examined Marsha. "Lots of blood on the floor. How bad was she?" He patted Penny's shoulder as he walked around her to see his patient better.

"Really bad." Jackie looked at Penny and then at Quinn. This wasn't the time to get into specifics. Penny's eyes still appeared haunted.

He nodded. "I need to exam her human side if that's possible. We're too far from a dual-natured clinic to work on her in this form. I'll use the human supplies they have here." He opened drawers filled with instruments she had no idea how to use.

"Hello Renee, thank you for assisting my mate in remaining safe," Quinn said in an off-handed fashion.

Renee smiled and nodded.

Quinn washed his hands and tried to keep them from trembling. The high levels of energy in this room scared Ramos and Antwan. The two opted to go to Nionis, grab the pups and leave rather than face La Patron. Since his mate's energy was the same as before, Quinn assumed La Patron had merged with Renee.

The energy spiked.

Marsha gasped and curled on her side, shivering in human form on the table.

Quinn cursed when he saw what they'd done to her and forgot about La Patron. "Craig, Penny, go get something to eat in the other room. We need to work on Marsha."

"No. I'm staying with her," Penny said, her mouth set in a stubborn line.

Quinn placed the needle, thread, gauze and other things he needed on the small table next to the bed. "As soon as I'm done you can come back. Go now. Not asking. I've got work to do."

Jackie extended her hand to Penny who took it and walked out while looking over her shoulder at Marsha. Quinn cleaned and reopened some of the cuts that had begun healing wrong.

Marsha screamed when he popped her bone back in place. Jackie returned and looked at him.

"Hold her for me, if we don't set this right she won't have the full use of her arm." He refused to think of the assholes who did this to the young pup, not now, later he'd get a name or description for Antwan or KnightForce.

With his mate assisting, the meticulous work on Marsha was easier. After a few minutes, she knew the names of the instruments he needed and had them ready before he asked. "*I wish our mental links were back,* "he thought.

I heard that," Jackie said with excitement. "*Say something else.*"

In a few hours, I plan to ride you so hard with my dick you'll be too tired to run into danger again. "He winked at her pinked cheeks. *Did you hear that?*"

Yes perv. Our links are working again."

Does this mean your dad saved the day? "He hadn't wanted to ask but couldn't help it now that they were almost done with Marsha.

Saved the day? Depends on your definition and who you speak to. Could we have disabled or taken out those three upstairs? Yes. "She pulled out her pouch of blades and showed him the sharp edges. *I'm really good with these. So is Renee. Nionis is just an all-out fighter. But we'll never know because my dad refused to take a chance and demanded we stand down.*"

Quinn didn't know what to say. She sounded pissed but he wasn't sure.

The only reason he didn't ride shotgun with me instead of Renee is I'm mated. I don't think he wanted to chance seeing anything." She grinned.

He said that? "Quinn asked as he finished stitching a large gash in Marsha's thigh.

No, he wouldn't admit that. Will she be okay?" Jackie rubbed Marsha's forehead. "*She's hotter than normal.*"

Her body's fighting for survival, the extra heat's normal. "He wiped his hand and looked at the young wolf. *Those bastards need to be strung up for this. She's just a pup.*"

Agreed, "Jackie said. "*You didn't answer my question. Will she be okay?*"

Physically? Yes. Not sure about mentally. She needs to be at the ranch with Ramos. He glanced at Renee. *Is that possible?"*

Jackie exhaled. *I don't know. Everything happened so fast. We haven't really talked. Plus, I'm pretty sure we'll need to have that conversation face to face.* Her gaze met his. *"He's not like you think or have been led to believe. Daddy's all about pack. He killed those rebels for kidnapping pups. My mom's pissed that Craig, Sean, Marsha and Penny has been victimized. She has a national group of women who watch over the pack and this is still happening. She's angry and wants to fix the atmosphere that allows this kind of thing to flourish."*

They want to talk to Ramos?"

Yes. And Antwan and the rebels they pulled in the woods. Kidnapping pups, breeding them at such young ages, the abuse, all of that has to stop," she said.

Quinn placed a clean sheet over Marsha's still, nude body and walked to his mate. Taking her in his embrace, he brushed his lips against hers. Her arms tightened around his neck as their foreheads touched. *"You sure you're not his ambassador? You got me believing,"* Quinn teased.

CHAPTER NINETEEN

Silas released a long sigh after saying good-bye to Renee and Jackie. His princess was indeed mated to a breed with a shadowy past. Quinn had heart and gumption, probably in equal measure because Silas hadn't learned much about the man even after searching Quinn's mind for answers. The insolent pup had locked every scrap of information down except his medical training. To pry further, Silas would've had to destroy Quinn to find out anything. He couldn't do that. No, he had to trust the Goddess and his princess regarding Quinn York and that rankled.

"All done? How'd it go?" Jasmine asked as she sat next to him on the sofa in their living room. He'd decided to deal with the rebels away from his office in relative comfort with his mate next to him. She passed him a tall glass of sweet tea and waited.

Appreciative, he patted her thigh, and took a long pull while gathering his thoughts. The silence in the room calmed and cleared the misty remains from Renee's colorful imagination and thoughts. Even while in a rested thought she read the world through a color palette, immediately noticing the ragged, beige and black dress the pup Penny wore, the clash of colors on the walls and floor. There had been so much minutia, he completely blocked her thoughts to focus on the rebels.

148

"Rebels." They were a constant thorn in his side, always had been but this, destroying and compromising pups... such young pups, left a hole in his heart. Somehow Marsha, Craig, Penny, Sean and the others fell through cracks he hadn't filled.

"Pups," he amended. "How am I still failing them?" He looked down at her, read the compassion in her gaze and looked away. Right now, he didn't need to be mollified. A pup almost died and he hadn't known of her existence. There had to be a way to better protect pups from rebels.

"Failing them? I thought you saved her life. What happened?" Jasmine asked.

Silas explained the events with the rebels, pups, Quinn and Jackie before looking at her again.

"We have a problem," Jasmine said, frowning. "No one abuses pack, especially pups."

"Agreed." Neither said anything more but he was certain she rolled through possible solutions just as he was doing.

"Sir, we're ready for the conference call," Hanks said through their link.

I'm in my suites, send it here."

Yes, Sir."

Silas told Jasmine about the call, together they walked into the den, activated the large wall screen and waited on the sofa. "Is this a good idea?" she asked.

"Hmm? What do you mean?"

"Talking to everyone except Jackie and Quinn, his uncle I mean," Jasmine explained.

"As soon as those two come up for air I want to talk to them face to face, but that's not happening now and we need answers. His uncle's been operating in Tennessee for over a century." Silas shook his head. "A century and I didn't know. How could we not know?"

"He saved a lot of lives," Jasmine said covering his balled fist.

"True... that goes a long way in making me feel better about all of this. Hopefully he can give us some ideas on how to stop the rebels." He paused, looked down at her and opened his link to help her understand how full of pride he had been earlier as he watched Jackie engage with pack.

"Sweet Bitch, you should've have seen her. Nothing we've ever taught or done for any of them could've brought her to that moment when she experienced the true pack dynamic. The look in her eyes as she picked up the pup, his affection for her and hers for him... it's what I want all of them to understand, to experience. Seeing her light up that way touched me in a way I can't explain."

Jasmine squeezed his hand and nodded. "Her mate exposed her to that. Maybe that's part of their connection. Him helping her find her voice, or mission. Think she'll go back to Houston?"

Silas shrugged. "I don't know. She never brought it up, everything was about the pups."

The screen flickered. Ramos, his mate, and Alpha Gilbert were on the screen. Gilbert immediately stood, the other two moved slower but the all bowed and greeted him and Jasmine.

"Sit, please sit. I appreciate you taking time to answer questions for us. First, this is my mate, Jasmine," Silas said.

"Hello La Patroness," Gilbert said. "It's been a while, and it's good to see you again."

"Same here, Gilbert. Wish it was under different circumstances. How is the pregnant young lady doing?" Jasmine asked.

Gilbert shuffled through a few papers. "Stable, and on bed-rest until delivery."

"Good. Thanks, Ramos and Antwan and you Gilbert for saving her life. It was extremely clever and well done," Jasmine said.

Ramos nodded but didn't say anything.

"Thank you, Ma'am," Antwan said.

"Also, I thank the two of you for rescuing and saving pups and pack for how long did you say?" She looked at Silas.

"Over a hundred years," Silas said the words bittersweet on his tongue.

"Wow, thank you. I know you didn't do it for us, nevertheless, we do thank you for your sacrifice. Is there anything we can do for you to help you continue this service?" Jasmine asked.

What are you doing?' Silas asked her.

"They're successful, we aren't. Not in this arena. We'll just back the winners on a case by case basis. After all this time, we

*know everybody's not going to join the pack but they need help
just the same. We give it to them in a way they can accept.
Nothing more or less,"* Jasmine said.

Ramos had been stuttering his surprise.

Antwan stared at the screen without saying anything.

"Sir, one thing they need is a fully equipped clinic or hospital
to help those who won't come on pack lands," Gilbert said. "From
what I've seen of the ranch it's large enough to build one on the
grounds." He looked at a stunned Ramos. "Do you think you can
staff it? Right now, you just have the one person working it, but if
it's larger, and modernized you'll need more staff."

Ramos stared at Gilbert and then his tortured gaze looked
directly at Silas. "I don't understand. You killed mam. You kill
those who disobey you. Why are you doing this when I refused to
register, and never took the pups who came through my ranch to
register." He frowned as if the math didn't add up.

Pack died for not registering?" Jasmine asked. The current
penalty was less severe even though some Alphas posted jail or
death if not followed.

"*Yes, when I met you in the hospital I ordered Tyrone's death
because he was unregistered. I changed it, but it had been the
law."*

"*This explains why many hide, instead of coming forward for
help and fall victims to the rebels, they still see you as that Alpha,"*
she said.

"*To an extent, I am that same Alpha,"* he said wanting her to
see him as he saw himself.

"*I could never have fallen in love with someone who killed his
own for a reason like that. You changed and I think you're a
better wolf for it. Based on what you've told me and what I've
seen, there will always be wolves who aren't comfortable in a
large, organized pack. They'll always be those who crave the
freedom of smaller groups and the wild. That doesn't make them
less pack, does it? Based on what the Goddess expects of you,
does it make them less pack?"*

No, it doesn't make them less anything. Uncertain of his
feelings on the subject, he turned and met Ramos' intent gaze.
"Who was your mam?"

"Arianna. She went looking for you and then nothing but her cursing you as she died."

Arianna again?" Jasmine sounded aggravated. *Should I tell him how crazy that woman was? What she did to Cameron? To Theron?"*

Silas watched Ramos. How much damage had the breed done to the pack over the past decades with his attitude against the Nation. What would happen if they relaxed the rules against joining pack further? How would Silas govern if he had no idea of the size and needs of his pack? Would that create more rebels? He wasn't sure and would discuss it with his brother, Angus and Jacques later. As Jasmine suggested, they could do this slowly with a few exceptions.

*I'm not sensing anger as much as confusion. The past is dead and Arianna is buried. If you think it's important to work with Ramos, we need to mend this breach, '*Silas said.

*We should work with him and his mate. No need to discuss that psycho bitch, '*Jasmine said.

"I recall Arianna. She threatened my mate and was guilty of a lot of crimes. But she did not die by my hands. She was in a tunnel that collapsed, it killed her." No need to mention the tunnel collapsed by his hand or that he would have strangled her if he had the chance.

Ramos nodded slowly. "I see."

"The law was relaxed after I discovered half-breeds living among us."

"Pardon me, Sir. But how is it you didn't know? We've been here for decades, centuries." Ramos rubbed his forehead with his fingers. "I'm having a difficult time understanding that you... La Patron had no idea of our plight. Of the infighting and bloodshed amongst us. Mam was passed around more than a pot of coffee for her ability to birth pups. She wasn't the only one either." He shook his head slightly. "I can't understand how you didn't know, didn't stop, what was going on."

A ball of fire pressed against Silas' chest. He released a long stream of air to ease the ache that never truly left behind this particular blind spot and failure.

Jasmine squeezed his hand and leaned into him offering comfort.

152

"I didn't know," Silas said slowly into the silence, adding nothing else. The infiltration of his pack by his enemies for so long was his greatest shame. Over the years, he tried to make restitution, but at the end of the day his ignorance of a festering cancer in his pack caused significant damage, and he still felt the fallout.

For several seconds, no one spoke.

"Goddess strengthen me," Ramos whispered, eyes wide as he continued staring at Silas and Jasmine. "You... you really didn't know?"

Silas shook his head. "No. Once I found out, we fought back on several continents. But until my mate stepped into the hospital to care for her son, I had no idea people like him existed."

Ramos sat back in his seat as if someone sucked the breath out of him. "All this time... I thought..." He wiped his face with his palm and closed his eyes. "Sir, I apologize."

"For?" Silas knew it was petty but since he'd just admitted his biggest sin he wanted Ramos to do the same.

"All the things I've thought and said about you. All this time I thought you ignored breeds, that you were a different version of the rebels who hate us but need us to remain relevant."

"That's harsh," Jasmine said.

"Again, I apologize, Ma'am. Decades of thinking a certain way will take a moment to readjust," Ramos said.

"Understandable," Jasmine said smoothly. "I like Gilbert's idea of building a clinic on your land for pack who won't come on pack lands. When you and your mate have time to think through it, contact Alpha Gilbert so we can make it happen."

"Yes, Ma'am," Antwan said while rubbing his mate's back.

"Does this mean Quinn didn't need to register in the database?" Ramos asked.

"Depends on why he registered," Silas said wondering where this was going.

Ramos smiled. "His mate asked him to do it."

Pride raced through Silas. His princess backed him even though Quinn had been taught against the registry. "In that case, I'd say he needed to do whatever made his mate happy." He picked up Jasmine's hand and kissed the back of it.

"Yes, Sir." Ramos paused, and cleared his throat. "There are a few things we feel can make life harder for rebels and keep pack safer."

"Like what?" Silas asked, listening intently. For the next hour they discussed strategy on how to curtail rebel activity in the mountains.

CHAPTER TWENTY

Taurus stared at the woman sitting across the desk from him and tamped down his anger. He'd been trying to contact the men sent to recover the pups and hadn't heard anything since they returned. He glanced at his watch and hoped this meeting would conclude soon. He planned to fly to Knoxville and spend time with Marsha and Penny.

"We're closer to getting this deal done, shouldn't be more than another 24 hours," Kristin Scott said from her chair in front of the desk. Inhaling, he sensed her fear. It wasn't of him, they'd been lovers long enough for him to recognize that particular strain. This was something different.

"Everything alright?" He tried to inject a modicum of concern in his voice when he wanted to cleanse the stench of her perfume from the air. Humans, especially those who thought then knew everything, disgusted and amused him. But they had their uses.

"Not really." She met his gaze directly. He liked she didn't back down, liked her drive and ambition. If she were a full-blood wolf, she'd be perfect. "Bradley's been acting strange lately, secretive."

"I thought you had his signature on the contract and it passed the legal department." As much as he enjoyed time with the delectable Kristin, if she didn't come through on her part of the deal, he'd snap her neck like a twig for wasting so much of his time. Time was one commodity he couldn't replace.

"Yes. Yes, that's done, the money should hit your bank in the morning and my offshore account." Frowning, she pursed her lips while looking toward the wall.

"So, what's the problem?" He didn't give a damn as long as the money he needed refilled his coffers. His pack needed supplies and food.

"Bradley's been acting strange lately, that's all. Normally he's not in the office but he's been staying late and refusing help." She snorted. "That's not like him at all."

"Does this impact me at all?" He wanted to catch that flight and deal with the traitorous bitch Marsha tonight before he bred Penny.

Kristin's eyes narrowed. "Only if he's poking around this deal you signed off on."

The words "so what?" were poised on his lips.

"He's a nasty bastard when crossed. He'd go public. Your face would light up the news and internet in a flash. If the company's buried like you said, and he's pissed, he won't stop digging," she warned.

"You knew this when you set the new woman up to take the fall?" he asked with grudging admiration.

"Of course, the bitch thought she could walk in and run my shop. Pity we lost Greenberg on that last contract, he was useful." She crossed her legs and he could see the light of cold calculation in her eyes. He wondered what patsy she used this time and promptly dismissed it. Over the course of their lucrative partnership she'd masterfully skimmed over a million dollars for him and he'd helped her in other ways, often resulting in bloodshed.

"You may need to take care of him," she said softly. "I'll let you know."

"I'm flying out of town tonight. I'll call you in the morning when I'm settled." They both knew he wouldn't, he never did but always said he would.

She stood with a slight smile tugging her lips. "If I didn't know what a stingy bastard you were, I'd be jealous you were using money from my hard work on another woman." She winked, turned and walked to the door. He watched the swing of her hips and inhaled her womanly scent.

His dick hardened and his beast howled. It had been three days since he'd sunk into her.

"Come here," he said stopping her as he unbuckled his belt. Fuck it. He would take a later flight.

CHAPTER TWENTY-ONE

Holding hands, Jackie and Quinn left the hospital after making sure Marsha was on the mend and Alpha Gilbert sent security for her safety. Nionis and Renee had returned to Nionis' home after taking the pups and the caregiver to the ranch.

Ramos and Antwan were meeting with Alpha Gilbert and Jackie was certain her father would talk to the men as well. She sent a quick prayer to the Goddess that the meeting would go well. She thought of Craig and hoped he understood why she wasn't at the ranch.

"Has Ramos had a chance to look into Craig's family?" she asked as they made their way to the jeep Ramos gave him to use.

"I'm not sure." He glanced at her. "Growing attached?"

Jackie cared deeply for the pup but wasn't sure what to do about her feelings. "In a way," she hedged before sitting in the passenger seat.

"Safe house?" he asked.

"Yes, Alpha Gilbert gave it to us for as long as we need it."

He nodded and pulled out the hospital parking lot. "When is your sister leaving?"

"In the morning, she has to go to work."

"What about you? When do you need to be back at work?" He glanced at her and then back at the road.

"I took this week off." She turned to face him. "We haven't talked about where we'll live or anything like that yet. What do you want to do?"

"How important is your work to you? You've never talked about it."

Which is your answer, she thought. "I enjoy the work. Mentally it's challenging and stimulating. I need that." Each positive point was checked and given weight.

"I'm sensing a "but" in there," he said after a few seconds of silence.

"Cons would be the people. Too much greed, insincerity and a level of viciousness that spins my head. Watching my back gets old after a while."

"To be fair, that happens in pack businesses too, just not as much," he said.

Since she had no experience with pack business she didn't comment on it. "Another con is the limitations placed on your abilities." She looked at him. "I was reprimanded for doing work I wasn't specifically hired for even though I have the skillset to do it." She shook her head. "They put you in these boxes so you don't contaminate anyone else."

He chuckled. "Where do you want to live?"

"With you," she said without thinking. "Wherever you are, I want to be there."

"Same here." He reached out, took her hand and squeezed. "I could go legit, practice medicine in the pack, work in a hospital or clinic. We could go where the need is the greatest to help."

Jackie's stomach clenched.

Earlier today she helped Quinn with Marsha, it was a great bonding experience but not anything she'd want to do on a continual basis. She needed the edgy work she'd done at the Pentagon or in her office for Mr. Bradley. Seeking patterns, truths, vulnerabilities fed her creative mind. Could she work in a clinic? She didn't see how.

"No?" he said. And to his credit he didn't sound disappointed or upset by her lack of response.

"Thinking about it," she said softly.

He turned onto the road of the safe house. "Just one idea. Being together is first. Doing what we both love doing is second." He pulled into the garage and turned off the vehicle. "We have time." He looked at her. "Right? We don't have to go see your parents or anything like that? Not right now, I mean," he clarified.

"Not today, but soon." She leaned forward and kissed him.

"Inside," he said on a husky note when they broke apart.

Everything tightened in her belly from the sound of his voice and his heated look. They entered the house, dealt with security and headed toward the basement. Before reaching the last stair, he picked her up, pulled her close and stared into her eyes.

"I know I haven't done anything that warrants you being in my arms, my life or my mate. But I'm so damn grateful someone with a heart and mind bigger than the universe chose me for you. I vow to show my appreciation every day of our lives. I couldn't have dreamed or imagined a better woman than you." His lips brushed against hers.

Shivery need wracked her body as he deepened the kiss. Arms beneath her ass keeping them close, mouths connected, he walked forward. Her back touched the cool surface of the wall. Unable to move, her grip around his neck tightened as he plundered her mouth. Breaking apart on a gasp, her chest expanded as she drew in much needed air.

"That was beautiful," she whispered trying to think of something equally poetic to say. "You're so perfect. Perfect for me."

He dropped his forehead to hers and took several breaths. "I want a thousand more sunsets with you."

Jackie closed her eyes to hold back tears as the realization, that even though she wasn't mushy or poetic, she really liked mushy, sunk in. "Me too."

He placed kisses all over her face, neck and shoulder. Tingles of need raced through her. Her core throbbed in anticipation of being filled. Her toes curled when he pinched her nipples.

"Quinn," she whispered pushing him back and sliding her palm against his chest. The need to feel his skin, the heated scent of her mate overwhelmed her. "Now."

Without another word he strode toward the bedroom and placed her gently on the bed. She missed his heat and scooted backward to make room for him. When he pulled his shirt off, revealing rock hard abs, a muscular chest and roped muscles in his arms, she stopped moving to watch. Holding her gaze, he toed off his shoes, and pulled down his pants.

His cock sprung free and slapped the bottom of his stomach.

"Breathe," she told herself as he crawled forward on the bed toward her.

Kneeling next to her foot, he removed her shoes and tossed them aside. Next, he slid both her panties and jeans down at the same time. She thought he'd take off her tee shirt, instead he leaned forward between her legs and kissed her heat.

Unprepared for his sensual assault, Jackie fell backward but placed one hand on the back of his head to hold him in place.

"Thank you, Goddess," he murmured as one finger entered her, and then another, stretching and ratcheting her pleasure.

"Oh, my god," she shrieked as suck and stroked in tandem, building, building unto she bucked upward and then flew over the edge. Her body shook as waves of pleasure rolled over her. Quinn's large palm rested against her belly, keeping her tethered to him.

Jackie took a deep breath.

Quinn slid upward and kissed her, hard. Initially she pushed back, not wanting to taste herself and then fell into the kiss, loving him, loving them. He positioned himself and slid into her tight sheath.

Nothing she'd ever learned prepared her for this level of connection. Colored ribbons rose above them twisting and turning with every stroke. She closed her eyes as a firestorm of intense need and pleasure erupted. He slammed into her as she lifted her hips to take him deeper, needing more.

"Close," he whispered.

Jackie couldn't talk and opened their link, and saw the ribbons now resembled a long braid. "Quinn," she screamed as she tumbled and spiraled into mind-boggling pleasure that crested higher and higher. Her walls clamped tight and released, over and over again until she was sure she'd pass out.

Quinn yelled, grunted, stiffened and finally collapsed on top of her.

Taking deep breaths to fill her air deprived lungs; Jackie lay beneath her mate, amazed by what happened. This time was different. Tiny shudders continued through her body re-validating they'd crossed into new territory. Her toes curled and then relaxed.

"That was unbelievable," she whispered.

He nodded. "You are."

She smiled and searched their link. "Did you see the colored ribbons?"

"Huh?"

"Colored ribbons, while we were doing it, the ribbons started twisting into a long braid." She looked down at the top of his head. "You didn't see it?"

"Don't think so. Nothing that formed anyway. I saw or sensed colors but no braid or anything." He rolled over, taking her with him. Her cheek lay on his chest.

"Hmm, interesting." She'd talk to her mom or Rose about it when she got home. The second the thought entered her mind she examined it. Was home the compound? Is that where she wanted to live? She could always find projects to help the Nation at the compound so that wouldn't be a problem. Matt needed help in the clinic and with half-breed research. Quinn would have his choice of work there. But is that what they wanted as a couple? She wasn't sure.

Yawning, Quinn pulled the blankets up over them, pulled her closer and kissed the top of her head. "I love this."

Jackie caught his yawn. "Me too." Listening to the steady beat of his heart, she fell asleep.

The ring of the phone pulled Jackie from sleep. Sitting slowly, she looked around the room for her jeans. Spying them on the floor at the end of the bed, she crawled forward and retrieved her phone from the pocket.

"Don't answer it," Quinn said laying his palm on her thigh and rubbing it.

"Could be Mama. She has to call when she wants to talk." Jackie frowned at the six missed calls from her boss.

"Is it your mama?"

"No, it's my boss. Strange cause he never called me before, someone always calls for him and never using his private cell."

"Yeah? Must be important, then." Quinn got out of bed. "Want something to eat or drink?"

Moving to sit beneath the covers, Jackie pressed the redial button. "A bottle of water and whatever you eat. Thanks."

He nodded and walked bare ass toward the kitchen, reminding her of the best night of her life. They'd made love three more times and the colored braid grew longer each time. Quinn never saw the braided ribbons and she stopped asking him about them believing it to be a female thing.

"Jackie," Mr. Bradley answered the first ring.

"Yes, Sir. Is everything alright?"

"No. Maybe. I'm not sure. Listen, did you talk to anyone else about the projects I asked you to review?"

"Just that one time with Kristin. We already talked about that." She paused. "What's wrong?"

"Can you return to Houston? It's really important or I wouldn't ask. Something's going on, I can't put my finger on it and I need your eyes. If it weren't so critical I'd send it to you, but I don't know who to trust."

He sounded paranoid and genuinely afraid.

"One of the reasons I took the time off was I got engaged. I'll talk to Quinn and let you know if we can cut our trip short."

"I'm so sorry and if you want a corner office after this I'll do it. It's just... I can't be losing my mind. I know what I saw and signed off on. I need to know what's going on and I trust you to tell me the truth."

Although flattered by his trust, she didn't understand. "Why? I mean, I've worked for you less than a year."

"This has been going on for a while but when you were here it stopped. Now it's happening again. That's why I trust you and not... some of the others. How soon can you come? I'll send the jet to pick you up."

"That won't be necessary."

"It is." He released a breath. "I've got papers, documents that I've mailed to your post office box in case anything happens to me. If and this is a big if, anything happens, nail those bastards."

Jackie didn't know what to say. "I'm sending security to watch you until Quinn and I arrive. Where are you?"

163

"I have my own security," he said. "Top of the line. Good security."

"Not like I'm sending. Don't argue, it's a waste of time. Where are you?"

She sensed his hesitation.

"This could be dangerous. Don't tell anyone at the company you're back. Just go to your box, get the documents and tell me what you see. I'll take it from there." He sounded more desperate.

"We can do that after I make sure you're safe." She grabbed Quinn's phone and tapped in Alpha Theron's private number.

"Jackie, I cannot drag you further into this. I accept I'm a target for trusting the wrong people but you don't have a bone in this fight. If you could just examine the documents and let me know if I'm right or wrong, that's all I need. My attorneys will take it from there."

"Why can't they verify your suspicions?"

He didn't answer.

"You don't trust them either?"

"They approved the documents you flagged."

"One second," she said and hit the mute button.

"Hello, Alpha Theron."

"Jackie, congratulations are in order I hear."

"Yes and thank you. Quinn is fantastic. I need a favor."

"Name it," he said.

She explained Mr. Bradley's situation and gave him the information she had on the man.

"We'll find him. Someone will be with him before you arrive. I'll contact Gilbert; the jet will be ready within an hour."

"Thanks." She explained to Quinn what was going on and he agreed they should go.

"Mr. Bradley, my fiancé and I are will return later today. I'll call you after I have the documents."

She heard something that sounded like a sob. "Thank you. I knew you were the right person to wade through this mess when I first met you. Please be careful and don't tell anyone what you're doing."

Obviously, he thought she'd made friends at the company. She hadn't. "Okay. I'll contact you soon."

Disconnecting the call, Jackie stared at her phone for a few seconds. It rang. This time Alpha Gilbert confirmed her need of the plane and gave her the time and place it would be ready.

Quinn had placed a bottle of water on the nightstand next to her. She opened it and took several large gulps. What was going on with Mr. Bradley? He sounded spooked. Quinn placed a platter of sandwiches and chips on the middle of the bed.

"Eat while I shower. I don't have clothes to pack. I'll buy what I need in Houston."

"I've got clothes at my house in Houston. I'll have Renee pack my stuff at Nionis' or leave them until we come back." She picked up a sandwich, and ate while tearing down Mr. Bradley's situation to look at it from several angles. It had to be one of the reports she submitted regarding acquisitions. Which one? She'd done five, only one was profitable.

Minutes later, Quinn strode out the shower, dressed in his tee shirt and jeans. He'd combed his wet hair back and looked so damn sexy as he slid into his shoes. Leaning across her, he grabbed a sandwich and winked. "Your turn. We can leave for the jetport when you're done and you can fill me in on the flight."

Jackie popped the last of her second sandwich into her mouth and headed to the shower.

Quinn admired the sway of his mate's hips and adjusted his hardening package. Now wasn't the time, although he was certain she'd always have that effect on him. He took the plate to the kitchen and finished his sandwiches.

Quinn?" his uncle said.

Surprised but happy to hear from the man, Quinn responded. *How's it going, Uncle?"*

Good, good. Better than I expected. Marsha's recovering. Penny's doing good, with all the security she feels safer and left Marsha's side last night to sleep in a pile with the others. The little ones are happy. I forgot to tell you we found Craig and two other parents. They'll be coming 'round to pick up their pups today and tomorrow. 'He paused. "*I had a conversation with La Patron, his mate and Alpha Gilbert. Scared me shitless but they were decent about everything. When will you and Jackie have a moment for us to talk?"*

Quinn explained they were heading out of town to Houston and he wasn't sure exactly when they'd be returning.

But you do plan to come back?"

Yes. But if you're asking if we plan to live here, I don't know. We haven't decided anything yet. 'He wanted to make sure his uncle understood he may not remain in Tennessee.

But you've started talking about it? 'His uncle pressed.

A little. 'He heard Jackie moving around the other room and glanced at the wall clock. *I'll let you know when we're heading back to Tennessee. We'll set something up."*

"*Sounds good. Be careful and watch your back."*

Will do, see you soon. 'Quinn watched his mate enter the room with a troubled look marring her forehead.

"What's wrong?" he asked as they headed toward the stairs and disengaged security.

"This whole thing with Bradley. Something's off. He has hundreds of people working for him, yet he wants me?' She looked at him. *What if this is a trap?"*

He frowned. "*Trap? For you? From humans?"*

She nodded slowly. "*I'll run it by dad, get his take on it."*

Quinn tamped down his irritation and didn't say anything while they drove to the jetport. They boarded and strapped in. Within minutes they taxied and took off. Jackie hadn't said anything since telling him she'd run to her father and he hadn't said anything either. The idea of his mate turning to someone else, rankled. No matter how often he told himself it was okay since it was her dad, it still bothered him.

Jackie touched his hand. He looked at her and heard her through their link. *There was a group, probably still is, who wanted to destroy my Dad and Mom. When we were pups, they poisoned our water, used chemicals in Nana's lotions that made us sick, sent in suicide bombers and a lot of stuff.* 'She waved her hand but held his gaze. "*It's not something that makes the papers or everyone knows about. Let's just say my father made sure we could defend ourselves against the crazies and those with legitimate challenges. All of us can kick ass with dad riding shotgun or not."*

"*Shotgun is what he did with Renee?* 'Quinn had wondered about that but forgot to ask.

166

She nodded. *Yeah, he can find us anywhere and assist or kick our asses. Same thing with my litter-mates, we can merge to share energy to protect ourselves.* 'She smiled. *What I'm trying to say is our enemies have used humans in the past to get at us, so we need to be careful. Having said that, I still plan to see this through. Cain, Abel and my dad all cleared Mr. Bradley, he should be good but if the right pressure is placed on him he could be perverted. That's why I wondered if it was a trap."*

Quinn processed as much of what she said he could. Cain and Abel he'd heard about. Seeing her father merge with Renee and the incredible energy produced by that would remain in Quinn's memory forever. He hadn't known of litter-mates merging or the problems or challenges La Patron and his pups faced. As a pup, he'd never been targeted or attacked. His uncle kept him close to the ranch, training him in survival tactics. Looking at his mate he realized life may not have been peaches and cream for her. *"Thanks for sharing and explaining. What did your father say?"*

I realized Alpha Theron or Gilbert probably already told him and he's already looking into it from his end. 'She waved her hand. *What do you think? Based on what I've told you about my job, how much extra security should we have?"*

Tell me more about your job, what you do and the people you work with? I'll answer after that, 'he said pleased she included him in her world and more importantly, she hadn't contacted her father.

CHAPTER TWENTY-TWO

Quinn watched the door of the private postal and shipping store for a few seconds before stepping out the car Alpha Theron provided from the private landing strip. Inhaling he sought the scents of nearby dual-natureds and even though Jackie warned him, he was surprised by their high numbers.

Lots of breeds and full-bloods live here." He looked at Jackie.

She shrugged and reached for the door. "*Work here if not live here. Don't forget Alpha Theron has security in place nearby and watching Bradley, which may be some of what you smell.*" She eyed him for a second. "*And don't forget I want to learn how to scent other dual-natureds while I'm human deep like this.*"

I won't. He knew how much she hated walking blind.

Let's go."

He removed her hand from the door handle and opened it. Once outside, he inhaled to see how close the dual-natureds were as he extended his hand to her. She took it as she stepped out. Quinn pulled her close against him and kissed the top of her head, his chin covered by her wild mane as he took another look around.

Embraced, they walked into the store and veered toward the mail boxes. Jackie pulled her key from her jacket, opened the box and looked at the slip of paper informing her she had a large package requiring her signature. She looked at Quinn and handed him the rest of her mail before heading to the counter.

"You have mail for me?" She handed the man the slip of paper she'd taken from her box.

He looked at it. "Yeah, I need to see your ID." He turned and walked to the back. A few seconds he returned with a large padded manila envelope. He pulled a piece of paper off and wrote her driver's license on it. "This is just for in-house," he explained.

"I appreciate that," she said giving him a smile.

The older man stared at her for a few seconds, glanced at Quinn's frown, and finished the transaction with a stuttering "thank you."

Jackie shook her head as they exited the store. *"You're bad."*

He stared too long."

I'm mated. No one will ever take me from you." She glanced over her shoulder at him.

"You and I know that. It's these other assholes I need to remind."

"Jackie? Is that you?" Kristin, the Sales Manager from her job asked looking at Jackie, then Quinn and then the store.

Quinn sensed his mate's distress spike and blocked the human's view.

Kristin craned her neck. "Jackie? That is you. When did you get back in town? Is everything okay? Mr. Bradley said you had an emergency." She moved to the side and watched Jackie.

This one needs watching," Quinn said. *She's been with a wolf."*

Damn it, I should've known," Jackie said tossing her mail onto the back seat. *Is it a scent you recognize?"*

No. But she's been fucked by one recently."

"I'm good, Kristin. Thanks for asking." Jackie slid into the back seat.

Quinn followed and closed the door in the woman's incredulous face. He sensed few treated her the way Jackie just did.

They remained parked in front of the postal store to see if Kristin went inside. A few seconds later she walked away.

"Have Alpha Theron assign someone to follow her. She's been with one of us," Jackie told the driver.

He nodded.

They pulled off and headed to her home. She picked up the hefty envelope and stared at the label. Next, she held it up to his nose.

"Papers?"

He inhaled. "Paper. Something plastic and metal. Maybe a disk. Nothing harmful unless it's the disk."

She released a held breath. "I don't want to be wrong about Bradley, but it's odd for him to beg me to return to look at this."

Based on what she shared about her job, Quinn thought the man had excellent insight and called the best person to help wade through this mess. He squeezed her hand and looked out the window as they entered a multi-lane highway. He couldn't imagine living amongst so many humans. And the bumper to bumper traffic was ridiculous. An hour had passed before they pulled off the freeway and headed toward pack lands.

"You did that every day?"

Jackie looked up from her reading her mail. *"What? Drive to work?"*

"Yeah, in that traffic, with all those maniacs?"

She laughed. *"I enjoy driving and it depends on the time of day. I go in early and miss a lot of it."*

He swallowed his disgust and sent a prayer to the Goddess that his mate didn't want to live in this horrible place. After clearing the gate onto pack lands, it took another 10 minutes to arrive at Jackie's home. She handed Quinn her keys and gave him the code while she spoke to the driver.

Quinn stood next to her and waited, ignoring her raised brow. Did she really think he'd leave her with another male, regardless of who he was? Together they entered her home and he shut off the alarm. Jackie continued forward down a hall and into a room. Quinn looked around on his way to the room she'd entered and appreciated her simple tastes in good, solid, furniture. Neutral wall colors warmed the room and made it more inviting to sit and rest. He looked forward to the two of them making love in this room later.

He entered what he assumed was her office. She sat on a long rust colored sofa looking at a disk drive. The contents of the envelope spread out in piles on the low coffee table in front of her.

"Can you start looking through this disk while I read these files? He highlighted a lot of things for me to look at," she asked as he moved further into the room.

"Yes." He extended his hand and looked around. "Which computer should I use?"

"Oh, one sec." She stood, walked to the desk and pulled out a laptop from behind a door. After turning it on, he gave her the disk to insert. "It's ready." She returned to the sofa, picked up the first stack and started reading.

Quinn watched her for a while and then opened the first file on the disk. Financials. He bit back a groan and did a cursory glance for anything glaring. If all these files were financials it was going to be a long night.

Jackie read Mr. Bradley notes and dug into the reports he referenced. It didn't take long to see why he assumed the worst. It looked bad but not conclusive. She continued digging through the data, putting pieces of the puzzle together to see the bigger picture.

"Did you call Bradley?" Quinn asked.

Jackie jerked and tore her gaze from the document she held. "What?"

"Your boss, did you call him? You told him you'd call," Quinn reminded her.

"No. I um... got distracted." She twirled her hair around her finger and continued reading a digital company's prospectus. Bradley had good instincts. Whoever put this together had been good, tiptoeing over the line on occasion but nothing too brazen. "What's on the disk?"

"Financials."

Another puzzle piece. "Company?"

"Yeah and a couple personal."

Excitement simmered as she walked to the desk, placed her hands on his shoulders and looked at the monitor searching for the digital firm. "Yes! Print these for me please." She pointed to the ones she wanted. "I need to see everything for that company."

Seconds later the printer spit out the pages. Taking them she did a quick glance looking for certain dates. "Who are the personal financials?"

"A. Johnson. K. Cross."

"Really?" She looked at the monitor again. "Didn't see that coming," she murmured.

"What?"

"Those two are the ones who were in the room when I thought I'd get fired. K. Cross is the woman who spoke to me at the post office, glad he didn't trust her. But A. Johnson is a senior VP and in line for Mr. Bradley's job. All this time I thought they were close."

"You changed your mind?" Quinn asked.

"Everything he's given me points to fake deals and money siphoned from the company to someplace else. Can't imagine he'd throw the records of his two top executives in this pile if they weren't involved somehow. He's looking for payoffs or something like that but they won't be here, not in the states anyway. I'd bet that. Let me finish this and I'll see if Cain will let us into his database."

"Cain?"

"Yeah, he trains the Knights and works at the Pentagon. He and Abel are the military liaisons for the pack. I interned with him and used their database for searches like these. He has to green light us using the system."

Quinn nodded. "Anything I should be looking for in particular in these files?"

Jackie returned to her seat. "No. Not really. Now that I understand who he's looking at, I'll sharpen my focus." She glanced at the numbers quickly and then at the documents she read before.

"Something to drink?" Quinn asked from the door.

"Yes, thanks." She didn't look at him but continued reading. "Son of a bitch," she murmured. Picking up her phone she placed a call.

It was answered on the second ring. "Jackie?"

"Alpha Theron where did Kristin go after we left the postal place?"

"One second." A few moments later he spoke. "She went to her office but returned to the store two hours later. She asked the guy at the counter about you but the guy who helped you had left work and another male was at the counter. She asked him if you'd picked up anything. He didn't know. She asked him to search the back to see if you signed anything. He claimed he couldn't access those records. From what I understand she was angry when she left."

Jackie shook her head. "Where did she go, then?"

"To a restaurant in Westbury."

"What?"

He chuckled. "To a small out of the way place. Good steaks I'm told."

"That's across town, easily an hour away with traffic. Did she meet anyone?"

"No. But she was on the phone a lot. She returned downtown and went to happy hour at a place near your office. Then she went home, alone. We're watching her tonight."

"Thanks. Her dealing with a wolf is a wild card. I don't know what that has to do with all of this or if she knows or not."

"No problem, I'm using this surveillance as a training opportunity for our security team. We don't interact with humans much but it's good to know how to deal with them when the need arises."

"Has Mr. Bradley left his place?"

"No. Hasn't answered his phone either. The human security company is pretty good, I know the company owner. If they miss something, we'll provide backup."

"Thanks, he was definitely onto something. I'll be contacting him soon. We'll need to set up a meeting to go over everything."

"Let me know so I can have security ready," Alpha Theron said.

"Will do, thanks." She disconnected and stared at the pages in her hand. "What are you doing Kristin? Are you and Johnson working together or separately?" Jackie wasn't sure.

Quinn returned with a bowl of chicken chowder soup and grilled cheese sandwiches. The savory aroma made her stomach grumble. She hadn't realized how long she'd been working or how hungry she was. He placed the plate in front of her and pulled a bottle of water from his pocket.

"Eat. Drink. Stay hydrated. Doctor's orders." He set the bottle on the table next to the plate, grabbed a sandwich and took a large bite. "We need to buy food."

Since she didn't cook often she never stocked her pantry. "You're right. After we meet with Mr. Bradley we'll stop on the way back here." She took a bite of her sandwich and looked around. "What do you think?"

"About?"

"My house. Renee helped with the decorations and kept it subtle. I wanted warmth and a sense of belonging."

"You've achieved that. I haven't seen much, but what I've seen is beautiful. But I'm not surprised." He smiled at her and finished eating.

Jackie stared at him a few moments. "I'm really lucky to have you." The surprised expression he wore pleased her.

"What?" he said.

She pushed the empty bowl aside and extended her hand. "I never went for fairy tales, the holes in them were too big. I mean a pumpkin? Lost glass slipper? A bite of an apple?" Appreciating his amused expression, she shook her head. "I'm digressing." She struggled to find the words to say how much he meant to her in such a short time. "If I did believe in fairy tales, you'd be my happily ever after," she said. "Since I don't believe, I feel like I'm living the reality and you're my prince and happy ending wrapped up in one." She mirrored his smile and released a nervous breath when his lips brushed against hers.

"My queen," he murmured and sat back. "How much more?" He looked at the pages covering the table and part of the sofa.

"Almost there. I'm going to call Mr. Bradley and set up a meeting."

"Good. Let me know if I can do anything to help." He stood, removed all signs of their meal and left the room.

Jackie placed the call to her boss. He answered on the first ring. "You're here?"

"Yes."

"Good. Are you okay? No problems?"

"No. Should there be?" She wished he'd tell her what else was going on instead of the cloak and dagger stuff.

"Maybe. I don't know. Have you picked up the information?"

"Yes. I've gone through most of it. Do you know about any offshore accounts?"

174

"I'm sure there are two at least. The security company I hired is looking into it." He exhaled. "Am I crazy? Seeing things that aren't there? Did I sign off on papers that could bankrupt the company?"

She hadn't gotten that far. "You're not crazy. There's definitely something going on. As far as bankrupting the company... I haven't seen anything that suggests that yet."

"Okay. It's hard being patient. Knowing that at any moment I can be arrested or taken in for questioning on these deals. I've had two others look at the deal you recommended we pass, after a few revisions they resubmitted it and it passed review. It's nothing more than a money-pit, a huge mistake. When I questioned Johnson about it, he claimed I insisted we go ahead with the deal even though he suggested against it. Somehow, it looks as if I've been buying and gutting companies, costing us millions. But I wouldn't have done that. I know I wouldn't have."

Jackie didn't move as several pieces of the puzzle slid into place. "Are you being blackmailed or something?"

"No. Not directly. Implicated in fraud and embezzlement. I've been relieved from my job pending an investigation," he said sounding tired.

She straightened in her chair and released a breath. "How's your health? Are you taking care of yourself?" She wondered if he was on medication and what kind he used.

"I get woozy sometimes."

"When do you want to get together to discuss this?"

"Get together?"

"Yes. I'm not going to talk about it over the phone." She assumed he'd want some type of covert operation to go over the facts.

"Right. Not safe. Let me think."

Jackie looked at the clock on the wall. She'd been at this for four hours and had a long way to go. "Call me after you and your team work things out."

"But you agree something's not right? I wouldn't have made these deals. No matter what's on those videos."

She groaned and shook her head. The dark pit grew deeper and wider. "Videos?"

He sighed. "The conference room has a recorder. We sign contracts there."

"You signed the contracts and now you're saying you didn't?" She didn't understand what was going on. This whole thing sounded like a bad movie.

Seconds passed. "I've been on very strong medication and at times I haven't been fully aware of things around me. I planned to retire for health reasons after this year and have been staying away from the office more and more because of... well my health."

"Who knew about this?" She hadn't noticed and that sucked. Quinn needed to teach her how to use her wolf skills while human deep.

"My assistant who's been with me for 20 years and Johnson. Just those two. Last week I learned he told others on the board and suggested the audit."

"Audit?" Jackie couldn't write a worst case scenario if she tried.

"Yes, it was completed the Friday before you left town. There's something wrong about all of this."

"Johnson and Kristin?" she asked.

"Maybe. But I'm not sure Aaron's guilty of anything other than concern for the company. Basically, he's a good man who feels awful about this."

Jackie snorted. "I want to see those videos. Do you have them?"

"Yes, my assistant has been wonderful. I have a copy of everything."

Quinn walked in, winked at her and returned to the desk.

"My fiancé is assisting me and he's wonderful too. As soon as we have a time for the meeting let me know. I have to make arrangements as well."

"Okay. And thank you for helping and not thinking I'm crazy or worse, a crook."

CHAPTER TWENTY-THREE

Quinn and Jackie nodded at the three, large human men who followed them into Mr. Bradley's home from the garage. Quinn and the security company finally came up with a plan of action to get Jackie and Mr. Bradley together. She held the leather satchel filled with copies of the paperwork he'd sent her. Back-ups of everything had been scanned and sent to the cloud she used for her Pentagon research.

Once Cain cleared her to use the secure database through his Department of Defense connection, she did a more extensive personal and financial search on Mr. Bradley, Mr. Johnson and Kristin. Fortunately, she hadn't found anything more on her boss, married and divorced twice with four Mistresses didn't count. Johnson and Kristin both had off-shore accounts with enough cash to retire anywhere in the world and live comfortably.

Jackie stood in the middle of either a family room or den located in the middle of the house. No windows and one door. Familiar stacks of paper littered a circular wood table in a corner. Two long leather sofas and two over-stuffed chairs were the only pieces of furniture. Unsure if they were supposed to sit and wait or if they'd be going to another room, Jackie looked around and then at Quinn.

His brow rose. *"Where is he?"*

Don't know. Pity you don't know his scent or how many heartbeats should be in the area. Otherwise...' she said.

Yeah, there are a lot of heartbeats nearby. I stopped counting at 10. Seems your boss really believes his life is in jeopardy with all this security, 'Quinn said taking the satchel from her, and holding her hand.

His professional life is in jeopardy for sure. I want to see the videos of him signing these contracts, something's definitely not adding up with all of this."

You believe him? That he's innocent? 'Quinn touched her chin, drawing her gaze.

You're going to kiss me? Here?"

He gave her a small grin. "*If I don't they'll think we're the oddest couple they've ever watched, standing, looking at each other and not talking. So yeah, I'm going to kiss you. If the old man doesn't come in here soon, I'll be doing more than kissing my fiancée.* 'Pulling her close, he swooped down and kissed her, stealing her breath.

Her arms crept around his neck as he deepened their kiss. His increased heartbeat and images of their time in bed last night or early this morning, replayed in their link. Her womb clenched in remembrance of his roar and her screams. They broke apart gasping and looking into each other's eyes.

Stop or I'll jump you right now," she told him breathing hard.

He pulled her close. *We won't do anything to embarrass you too much."*

She tucked her face into his chest, breathing in his scent to calm down. His heartbeat normalized and she synced hers with his. Inhaling deeply again she shivered. *You smell so good. Like... like home with a healthy dose of sin."*

Quinn chuckled. Arms wrapped tightly around her, he rocked them from side to side. "*Sin, huh? I'll have to think on that. Time to say something. Just nod when I make a few sounds.* 'He leaned close to her ear and made meaningless sounds. She nodded and laughed when he bit her earlobe.

She pushed back but didn't leave his arms. Looking up she read the mischief in his gaze. "*What?"*

Security is completing their check on us, mostly me. Since they won't find anything, they're suspicious. How long do you want to wait around? 'He tapped the tip of her nose with his finger. So, beautiful, I'm a lucky man."

"Yes, you are," Mr. Bradley said entering the room from behind them.

Jackie moved to Quinn's side to greet her boss. But the words stuck in his throat. Less than seven days had passed since she'd last seen him and either his suits did a masterful job of hiding his lean frame before or he'd lost considerable weight. She wasn't sure which.

"We're both lucky," Jackie said when she found her voice. "How are you, Mr. Bradley?"

The old man's brow rose. "How do I look? The picture of health? Or like a man who knows he's next on list of targets who've gone missing?" He grunted and then started coughing.

Jackie glanced at Quinn who watched Mr. Bradley. "*He knows. I came to the same conclusion in my research. Several of the principles who were loaned money are missing, possibly dead. He looks bad.*"

Is this how he looked when you saw him last? 'Quinn asked.

No. But I've never seen him dressed in a jogging suit either. Maybe he's always been this... slim."

Hmm. Human murders are a constant refrain in history. Money is often at the root of it. If you choose to work in a company, we'll start our own to avoid that."

The old man sat on the sofa and waved at them. "Sit. Sit. I want to know what you think." His glance shifted from Jack to Quinn and back to her again.

"What's wrong with you?" Jackie sat on the sofa across from him and scooted forward with her hands clasped tight. Quinn walked to the entrance and leaned against the wall.

Mr. Bradley waved off her question. "Too much to go into now. Surgery will take care of most of it. But that's after I clear my name. What did you think of the documents I sent you? The missing people and money?" He crossed his legs and held his knee just as he had in previous board meetings.

"Two companies you signed off on are bogus, money pits. Company funding to those firms disappeared shortly after the ink was dry. I agree its suspicious the primaries in those companies also disappeared." She continued going through her findings, answering his questions and asking a few of her own.

"I'd like to see the videos of you signing the contracts," she told him when she'd gone through her analysis.

179

Mr. Bradley nodded and looked over her shoulder. The room dimmed slightly as a panel against the wall behind Mr. Bradley lowered. Moments later the conference room where she'd sat in many meetings came into view. The door opened, Mr. Bradley, Mr. Johnson and three men she'd never seen before entered.

"This is the digital company," Mr. Bradley said.

Jackie watched the signing. *"What do you think?"* she asked Quinn.

"Nothing stands out as wrong to me. You?"

No. Which means there's a problem. He signed these contracts with no influence."

Now he's having buyer's regret?"

"Could be. I don't know. We're missing something."

"This is the other one, the one you turned down was revised and resubmitted," Mr. Bradley said.

Jackie nodded. The camera showed Mr. Bradley, Johnson and one man enter. *"Whoa. That's Jonas. The wolf who asked me to intercede on a contract,"* she told Quinn.

Which contract?"

I don't know. I said no and dismissed him. Haven't heard from him since. The contract they're signing is the same contract Kristin was upset about. Is it possible Jonas is the wolf you smelled on her?" More pieces of the puzzle fell into place.

Anything's possible. I don't recognize him. Ramos may know him. I'll ask."

"Can we get a close up of the man in the pearl gray suit?" Jackie asked Mr. Bradley.

"Jonas Gray?"

"I want to see his face," she said as the camera zoomed in on Jonas. "I want to run his picture by someone."

"You know him?" Mr. Bradley asked watching her closely.

"No. But he approached me at lunch one day, asked if I'd have dinner with him. Claimed he wanted to talk to me about something. At dinner, he said a contract hadn't gone through, I told him I couldn't help him without ever learning which contract or anything else. I dismissed it. He left. I finished dinner. This happened the same day you called me in your office regarding Kristin and the contract you dropped. I wonder how he knew

180

what to do to repair the contract? And how did he know I'd worked on it?" She met his gaze.

"Kristin Cross." Bradley shook his head. "This is how women get a bad name in business circles. She makes six figures with all the perks, why sabotage the company?"

Jackie didn't know and remained silent for now regarding his comment on women getting a bad name about the same things men did all the time. "*A full-blood being involved changed things, especially with humans disappearing. I have to inform Alpha Theron since it happened in Texas,*" she told Quinn who agreed. Theron would inform her dad. "Fortunately, the amount he received was significantly less than the digital company who required more for equipment."

"We're tracking them down and should have that locked down by tomorrow. We haven't been able to locate the Gray fella. Kristin hasn't been with him since we signed."

One of the big men entered the room holding Jonas' picture. Quinn took a picture of it on his phone and sent it to Ramos. "*I may need to record the video on my phone and send it to him so he could see how he moves, maybe hearing his voice will help.*"

Jackie nodded.

"What about Aaron Johnson? How involved is he?" Mr. Bradley asked handing her a few papers

She shrugged, took the pages and read the first one. "He has money stashed away but the dots aren't as clear to him as they are with Kristin."

"*Shit,*" Quinn said.

"*What?*" Jackie looked at him staring at his cell.

Jonas Gray. He's Taurus. Jonas Gray is Taurus, the rebel leader. This must be the deal to get extra money he'd been working on."

Jackie rubbed her forehead. "*Jonas and Taurus?*"

Not and, they're the same person. Ramos thinks he's headed for Tennessee to get Penny but she and Marsha are staying at Alpha Gilbert's compound for now."

Great."

Did Jonas know who you were? La Patron's daughter?"

181

Jackie thought about how he entered the restaurant and remembered she'd wondered how he found her since she'd been human deep. "Yes, he did. He knew I was pack. Tango was there."

He stole money for the rebel's cause from a company where La Patron's pup worked, approached you and asked for your help. Bold bastard, Quinn said.

I don't think this is a direct attack against La Patron. If he recognized me, that was an added bonus. I wonder how he gained Kristin's help or is this all her idea. Why would a full-blood pick that company unless someone on the inside assured him it could be done? Maybe she's been doing this for a while and he took advantage of what was offered.

Possibly." Quinn didn't seem convinced. *Ramos wants to be kept posted. He informed Alpha Gilbert.*

I informed Alpha Theron and sent him a picture of Jonas. Tango had reported the initial meeting so they have preliminary information on Jonas already. His men are surrounding this building and will look for Jonas if he approaches. If he had anything to do with the missing men, Theron will take over and handle him."

A phone rang.

Jackie looked at her boss.

The door opened and a tall man she hadn't seen before entered. His gaze zeroed in on Mr. Bradley. "You aren't supposed to have a phone," he said in an accusing tone.

"It's one of those throw away ones, can't be traced." It rang again. "It's a trap. Only gave the number to Kristin and Aaron."

Jackie bit back a caustic remark about people playing James Bond in real life situations. Jonas' involvement ratcheted the tension and involved KnightForce as well as Alphas Gilbert and Theron's security. Things could go bad quickly.

"Hello," Bradley answered sounding more like his old self.

Jackie marveled at how upbeat he sounded on the phone before he frowned and his face whitened further. "What are you talking about?" He looked at the phone and at Jackie. "Kristin wants to talk to you. She says what happens next is your fault. Something about Jonas not stopping."

Before Jackie could take the phone, Quinn grabbed it. "Hello?" He paused. "Yes, this is him. She's in the bathroom." Quinn held Jackie's gaze and opened their link.

The next second the house shook as glass shattered and smoke exploded. Quinn dove forward, covering most of Jackie as the roof caved in.

Bradley screamed and then went silent.

Jackie's world went dark.

CHAPTER TWENTY-FOUR

Quinn shrugged off the wood and drywall from his back. Sounds of groaning, yells in the distance and stirring filled the air. Through the dust and debris, he saw Jackie lying beneath him.

Jackie?" he called through their link. Nothing.

A large beam and wood had created a small cave-like area protecting them from being crushed. He inhaled. Fire. He touched his mate's shoulder to awaken her and saw the large gash on the side of her head where her skull had been crushed. A tidal wave of fear washed over him. He needed to get her someplace to work on her wound. He crawled beneath the beam, stood slowly and tried to move the wood.

It wouldn't budge. Spirals of smoke slid into the area near Jackie.

Desperate, Quinn summoned his beast, and pushed harder on the beam. It gave some but more dust and drywall fell onto Jackie covering her upper body, making her appear ghostlike.

He stopped moving the piece, crawled to his mate and pulled her next to him while wiping off the dust. Once her head was protected, he moved the beam.

Smoke filled the room.

184

The sky appeared through a large gaping hole in the ceiling. Sensing the fire growing stronger, Quinn cleared a path to the door but stopped at the entrance. Bodies lay unmoving, covered in dust beneath parts of the house. Some were consumed by the blaze.

He retraced his steps and checked the side of her head. The gash wasn't as bad but seeped blood. Picking her up, he headed to the doorway. In the hall, he made his way toward the rooms in the opposite direction of the fire.

Although this part of the house hadn't taken a direct hit, he feared it would falter beneath the weight of holding the remaining structure in place. Fire licked and consumed the entry and garage. At the end of the hall Quinn kicked opened a door and released a pleased sigh at the bed undisturbed in the middle of the room. Over his shoulder he noticed smoke creep down the hall as if following him.

He shut the door with his foot, laid Jackie on the bed and searched every drawer and closet for a first aid kit or something to clean her face and wounds before her skin re-knitted. Cursing the lack of a attached bathroom and empty closets and drawers, he tore strips from the sheet and wiped her face.

Smoke curled beneath the door. A loud crash split the air. The house shuddered. They had to leave.

He opened the window and looked down at the steep cliff filled with rocks and fallen logs. It was at least a eight feet, maybe more, drop and would no doubt kill a human. Quinn kicked out the window, picked up his mate, held her close to his chest, and after calling his beast, jumped. They rolled and came to a stop against a large rock.

Every place in his body hurt from taking the brunt of the fall. Pebbles and rocks cut into his skin like sharpened blades. Wiping his mouth to remove debris, he took a moment to bring much needed air into his lungs. Maybe they could stay here for a few moments, wait for the Alpha's men.

"Jackie?" he called her name repeatedly, desperate to hear her voice, to know she was okay.

Nothing.

His head dropped for a few seconds as despair choked him. He couldn't lose her, not now, not ever. Inhaling, he banished the dark thought as he moved closer and saw the gash to her head seep fresh blood. He clamped down on the howl of anguish rising from his throat and picked her up. She needed medical attention now.

A burning sensation slammed into his arm, spinning him and sending him to his knees. He held onto Jackie and looked at the hole in his shoulder. Another bullet whizzed by his ear and he ducked down. Where the hell were the Alpha's men? He lay Jackie down and felt the back of his shoulder.

Relieved the bullet went straight through; he reached out to Ramos and told him what happened. *"Pull up a map, we flew into El Paso, drove about 45 minutes, came down a long dirt road, a stream runs through the property, uneven terrain, I can see a couple hilltops, lots of trees. He built the house in a clearing which makes it easier to get picked off."*

'Are you trying to get to El Paso?"

'That may be the closest hospital.' With Jackie close to his chest he eased backward, down the cliff. Hopefully it wasn't a dead end. The wound in his shoulder throbbed. He ignored it and kept going.

'Okay. I'll also pass this along to Gilbert. They'll be all over this. Can you hide somewhere until they get to you?"

Hiding went against every fiber of his beast but his mate hadn't stirred. He couldn't risk her wound getting worst. Smoke billowed from the window opening he'd jumped through. Heat singed his lungs. What if it did the same to his mate? That would mean she suffered from a blow to the head, possibly twice and smoke damage. Which was worst? Remaining here inhaling damaging smoke? Or using the smoke as cover to run so she could breathe clean air? Both options sucked. If the shooter hadn't used a silencer, the Alpha's men would have him or them by now.

'The smoke is too thick I need to move.' He opened his senses. There were a lot of full-bloods and a couple humans nearby. Holding Jackie close, he picked his way back up and cleared the small ravine. He moved toward the full-bloods.

"This way," one called from the side.

Unable to see clearly through the thick smoke, Quinn followed the full-blood up and out of the smoke into a copse of trees. *We have some help with a full-blood,* he told Ramos what happened.

Great. I'll pass it on."

Once they were in a clearing, Quinn inhaled deeply to clear his lungs.

"Do you need help with her?" He reached for Jackie.

"No." Full-bloods knew better than to touch another's mate. He looked at his rescuer, the man looked familiar but Quinn couldn't place him.

"What happened?" the full-blood asked looking at Jackie.

Another red-flag. Alpha Theron would've told his pack members what he wanted them to know, they wouldn't ask him questions. There should be more of them. *"Ramos, I think we have a rogue wolf.* He turned so that Jackie wasn't in the wolf's view and lay her down gently.

"Someone shot something into the house and it exploded," Quinn told the wolf as he prepared to attack.

"Good thing we came along and the two of you got out safely. Alpha is happy about that."

Quinn turned and saw the full-blood holding a gun. Rather than ask questions, Quinn leapt forward, morphing mid-air, ignoring the fire spreading through his leg as the bullet ripped through. Intent on destroying the threat to his mate, he crushed the arm the full-blood threw up in defense and went for his throat.

The full-blood shifted.

Quinn was on him, fighting through a red haze of rage that wouldn't release him. They charged and fought on hind legs, each seeking the advantage. Snarls filled the air as Quinn went after the wolf with single-minded determination until he snapped the neck of the bastard threatening his mate. When the wolf lay prostrate beneath him Quinn backed up as others formed a half circle around them. He stood over Jackie snarling his threat against any who would hurt her.

"Easy, I'm Theron, Alpha of Texas. We're here to help, I promise. My word, she's safe." The tall barrel chested, full-blood with long dark hair extended his hands in a peace offering. His gray eyes changed to a bluish-green similar to Jackie's.

Quinn recognized La Patron's energy and remained near his mate.

A few men went to move the dead full-blood. Quinn growled.

"Leave him for now," Theron said watching Quinn who looked down at Jackie and licked her face.

Quinn morphed to human and stared at the men. "Do any of you have a first aid kit?"

"Someone will look at those bullet wounds as soon as we get you out of here. The human police and fire department are on the way here. I can't keep them away much longer," Theron said.

"Not for me," Quinn snapped and picked up Jackie. "For my mate. She's been hurt." He ignored the blood seeping from his wounds and stared at Theron expectantly.

"I'll get you one. Please come with me, we need to leave this place." Theron waved him forward.

Quinn looked at the dead wolf on the ground and it clicked. "Johnson."

"What?" Theron said walking beside him without touching Jackie.

"The dead man is Aaron Johnson, he worked at the company as Vice President or something similar," Quinn couldn't recall exactly. "Jackie didn't know he was a wolf."

"In sheep's clothing," Theron muttered as they entered a black SUV.

Quinn held Jackie close on his lap and kissed her forehead. *"Come back to me. I need you. Please come back to me."*

Nothing. He lowered his forehead to hers and rocked gently. *Please come back to me. Wake up, Jackie. The world's too dark without you. I need you as much as the air I breathe."*

The SUV raced over uneven terrain, the jolts reminded him he'd been wounded. They all breathed a sigh of relief when they reached a paved road and could make better time. Minutes later they entered a gated area and pulled into a parking lot.

"One of our clinics," Alpha Theron said as he slid out the passenger side and opened the door for Quinn. Holding his precious mate close, Quinn moved quickly through the doors, pleased to see a team waiting for them.

"This way, Doctor," one of the men said.

Quinn followed them to a room and placed his mate gently on the bed. He removed her clothes, washed and examined her at the same time. The gash to her head concerned him the most. It appeared to have healed. He worried about bone fragments from her skull being embedded in her brain which could cause all types of problems. He ordered several tests and stood by as each one was completed.

A blue-eyed Theron remained next to him the entire time as he reviewed the test results. She should be awake. Her brain scans and every other test came back clean. There was nothing to explain her being out this long.

Quinn looked at Jackie lying on the bed, and took her hand. Closing his eyes, he sought their link and called. *Jackie. Jackie, where are you?* Waiting for a response, he sought his mate. *Jackie there's nothing medically wrong with you. How can I help you come back?"* He waited. A thought occurred to him. *We need you to finish this puzzle, Johnson was more involved that we thought. I don't know how I missed it."*

Litter-mates. Her words floated toward him.

Quinn exhaled and bowed over in relief.

I don't understand. What about your litter-mates? Are they coming? Is Renee alright?"

Hurt... Brothers... Never mind... Her words made no sense. Was she hurt? Or her brothers? What was going on and why didn't she wake up?

What kind of help should I find? Your father's here with Theron, does he know what you're talking about?" he asked frantic to understand.

No... Quiet place we go.... Almost done," she said.

Quinn didn't know what to say about that. In a way, he felt slighted that the four of them had a mental oasis to hide and get refreshed while he'd been left fighting for their lives. *I'll leave you to it, then."* He pulled out of their link, opened his eyes and met Theron's bluish gaze.

"She's alright?" Theron asked.

"Yes. She's been with her litter-mates. Excuse me." Quinn left the room and went to an empty examining room. He shut down his link to block his thoughts as he removed his shirt, and unwrapped his shoulder. The bullet left an angry mark but it

189

seemed to be healing. He rotated his arm a few times and then unwrapped his calf.

For a few seconds, he stared at the reddish-brown wound in his leg. All this time she'd been hiding somewhere in her mind, ignoring him. He couldn't believe it. Through the smoke and collapse of the house, she'd refused to return to him. He closed his eyes briefly to shut out the mind-boggling fear that gripped him earlier of not protecting her. Until now he hadn't dealt with how close he had come to losing her or them both dying.

The door opened behind him.

Quinn straightened and didn't turn to face Alpha Theron.

"I don't want to like you," Theron said.

Quinn knew the words were La Patron's and didn't respond. Instead he bent forward and poked the wound on his calf.

"My mate thinks it's because I see a lot of me in you. I don't think so but... she's been right more than wrong so who knows."

Quinn looked over his shoulder at the man and then returned to tending his wound.

"Since my mate doesn't want us to fly to Texas to interfere, I'll need to speak with you through Theron unless you give me access to a link between us."

Quinn heard the hopeful tenor in the statement and realized he didn't want anyone else to know what happened with his mate. He hesitated for a few seconds. Once he allowed La Patron in it was permanent. But so was his relationship with Jackie. "We can link," he said and prepared for the link to materialize. He locked down everything just as La Patron appeared.

"I'll be in Jackie's room while the two of you talk," Theron said as he left.

Quinn nodded.

A second later heat raced through his body. He shuddered from the intensity and crumpled to the floor shaking. Fire surrounded the bullet holes. He bit down on his lip to stop the scream of pain from erupting. Beads of sweat popped on his forehead as he continued trembling beneath the assault. A breeze flowed down their link and spread through his body in a weird cooling sensation Quinn never would've believed possible. As the pain subsided, he watched the mark disappear on his leg. A quick look at his shoulder showed no bullet hole.

Impressive. Jackie had been right thinking her father could heal the pregnant girls.

Now we can talk without you being distracted."

Quinn nodded and realized La Patron couldn't see him. *Okay."*

You're upset Jackie went to her litter mates when she was in trouble?"

Is that what happened?" Quinn had never heard of anything like that before, didn't know it was possible. She mentioned sharing energy but a quiet oasis?

In a way. They're close. When they were pups, we suspected they spoke mind to mind at an early age. There's not a lot of information on half-breeds so we didn't know what was possible and what wasn't. This may be normal. We're watching the others to be sure, so parents will know what to expect."

Quinn didn't know what to say. La Patron knew his pups were together but he wouldn't help Jackie wake up? Or was the message Jackie gave him so garbled she wasn't with her litter-mates?

"*Tyrese and Tyrone, my two oldest sons are also breeds and can share each other's energies, thoughts, and can link so tight you can't separate them. They can find each other no matter where, it's amazing what they're capable of as litter-mates."* La Patron sounded proud.

Are they mated?" Quinn wondered how this impacted their mates.

Yes. There was a problem with Rose, Tyrone's mate. He and Tyrese were linked in such a way; they both thought she was their mate. My mate solved the problem by making them separate completely. Tyrese is mated to Danielle. They all have pups."

Quinn didn't care about any of that. His mate zoned out on him at a critical time and refused to acknowledge his pleas to return. That part hurt the most. He needed to be first with her and he wasn't.

When the two of you visit, you'll meet them."

Okay." Quinn refused to discuss what he deemed as a serious communication problem between him and his mate with her father.

191

My mate's better at this family stuff and wants me to welcome you to the family. Call me Silas in private, not dad or anything like that."

Okay.' Quinn hoped to avoid conversations with the man as much as possible and the idea of calling him dad never occurred to him. Standing, he grabbed his shirt as he left the room and returned to Jackie who lay peacefully on the bed.

Theron clapped Quinn's shoulder. "If you need anything, just ask. I have them bringing you a meal and exchanging the bed for something bigger so the two of you can rest."

"Thank you, I appreciate it," Quinn said with heartfelt gratitude.

"No worries. The pups are well-loved in this state." He walked out leaving Jackie and Quinn alone.

Quinn sat on the side of the bed and stared at his mate for a few seconds before crawling in next to her. Holding her close he wondered what kind of relationship they'd have if she could leave him so easily.

CHAPTER TWENTY-FIVE

"Ow," Adam yelled through the link all four pups shared. "What's going on?"

"Wake up, Jackie," David said sending energy through their link to revive her.

"What's wrong with her?" Renee asked as she sent energy toward her sister. Soon all three sent healing energy to their fallen litter-mate.

Jackie groaned.

"That hurt," Adam said. "Like someone hit my forehead with a wooden baseball bat."

"Let her catch her breath first," Renee said.

"What... Quinn? Where's Quinn?" Jackie asked trying to look around. Instead she saw her litter mates in the small den they created as kids. "What are we doing here? Where's Quinn? Something's happening. I need to get back to help."

"That's a good question," David said.

"Which one?" Adam asked rubbing his forehead. "The one about Quinn or what happened? I vote for what happened."

"Neither," David said. "What are we doing here? We haven't linked to this place in years."

"Can we talk about this later?" Jackie said, desperation to return to her mate coated her words. "I need to get back to Quinn."

"Go," David said. "I'm not stopping you." He looked at Renee. "Are you stopping her from leaving?"

"No. I'm trying to get back to my painting. I'm at a delicate part of the design or I was until I felt Jackie's pain. For some reason, I was pulled here like the rest of you," Renee said.

Jackie looked at Adam.

"I was taking a nap."

Renee snorted.

"I'm going out later and need to be on my game," Adam said. "But it's strange we're here. Especially you, Jackie. I didn't think mates could be separated like this. Not that you told me or David about your mate."

"Sorry, guys. I planned too, things spiraled and the mating heat's no joke." She smiled at him. "His name is Quinn York, a doctor who has a heart for pups. He lives in Tennessee, I met him while visiting Nionis and I need to get back to him."

David opened his arms and she accepted his strong, warm embrace. Next, Adam hugged her. She stepped back. "Thanks for the healing energy guys, it was a hard blow." She pointed to her head. "We're coming to see Mama and Daddy soon, you'll meet him then."

"Will you have a mating ceremony like Vanessa and Ethan?" Renee asked with an eagerness that made Jackie pause.

"I don't know about a full wedding. We'll let you know," Jackie hedged. Anxious to help her mate she tried to wake and couldn't. Closing her eyes, she sought the link with Quinn without success.

"Why can't I go back to my painting?" Renee asked, her voice rose on the last word.

"I can't wake up," Adam said looking at each of them.

"Where's my link with Quinn?" Jackie asked frowning.

"None of my other links are working," David said.

Jackie and the others stared at him. She reached out to Nionis, her father, Cain, Quinn again and sagged against the wall. Trapped in their links? How was that possible? "This isn't good or normal. I'm mated for Goddess sake. We can't be separated."

She looked at her siblings, hoping one of them had an answer. They all looked just as confused as she felt.

David walked toward one of the four large overstuffed chairs in their space and sat. Renee and Adam followed suit. "We have a problem," David said what had to be the biggest understatement of the century in Jackie's opinion.

Rather than say anything unhelpful, Jackie nodded.

"A big problem," Adam said. "You guys built this place after dad taught us how to find, I think he called it solace, within ourselves when we have problems. He said it kept him centered for centuries until he found mom."

"I remember linking with Jackie to create a quiet space where I could paint and she could work on her stuff away from the noise in the nursery." She stared at Adam.

"We were kids. Kids play and get noisy sometimes," Adam said grinning. "I try not to be as noisy now, I can't always vouch for my dates."

"Yeah, that was the reason we did this," Jackie said remembering and ignoring Adams' comments. "Later, I pulled David in to help with a debate I was working on."

"He pulled me in sometime after that," Adam said. "But we've always been able to leave."

"We've never almost died like Jackie did earlier. Her pain went through all of us, and pulled us back here," David said slowly as if picking his way through rocky process.

"Wait," Adam said sitting forward. "If one of us gets badly hurt we get dragged here to heal? Until when?" He pointed at Jackie. "She looks better to me."

The three of them looked at Jackie. "How do you feel?" Renee asked.

Jackie thought about it for a few seconds. "Better. Actually, I don't feel anything. Are you still feeding me energy?"

"Not intentionally." Renee placed her fingertips together as she leaned forward with her elbows on her knees. "But I sense a lot of combined energy flowing around here. Shouldn't it be getting weaker?"

"Who knows?" Adam said. "Who can we ask? We're the prototypes, remember?"

None of them said anything for a few moments.

Jackie felt a trickle of energy and sought her link with Quinn. He had to be worried. "*Quinn!? Quinn,*" she called out to him as the energy floated away. "I need to get out of here."

"Is your beast seeking your mate?" Renee asked.

The question made Jackie pause. "Not really." Which made this situation weirder. "I should feel discomfort from the separation, right?"

Renee held up her hands. "Don't ask me."

"I'm not asking, just making a comment," Jackie snapped.

"Chances are you aren't separated from him, maybe a temporary block in your link or something. Maybe it was open when you got hurt or something like that. I can't reach Sarita either and that's only happened a couple times," David said in an even tone.

No one would mention Sarita and David weren't mated or the time Sarita was kidnapped and David went off the rails ballistic, it was the one time she'd seen her normally unflappable brother out of control.

"Does that mean if I get hit in the head or have a bad accident, we get dragged here?" Adam asked bringing them back to the problem at hand.

"Or driving a car," Renee said.

David shrugged. "What we do know is one of us was dying and this is the result. If Jackie's body is still being healed with our combined energy, we can't tell. Maybe when she's out of the red zone we can leave," David said.

"Daddy doesn't know about this," Renee said, her gaze met Jackie's.

"Rese almost died when Rone was shot in the war," Jackie said thinking it through. "Rese saved his life." She looked at them. "Thanks, I appreciate your help." Why hadn't Quinn stepped in instead of her siblings? Wasn't that the way it worked?

"It's what we do," Adam said giving her a thumbs up.

"No, that's not what I meant when I said Daddy doesn't know about this and if we tell him, he'll keep us locked behind the walls of the compound forever," Renee said, a tremor in her voice.

"What are you talking about?" Adam said.

"Think about what's happening right now," David said looking at his brother. "Can you defend yourself? If you were on the

196

soccer field or driving a car or shopping and Jackie got hit with whatever happened to her, what would happen to you? How do we protect each other from this?"

"Damn," Adam said placing both his hands on his head as he leaned back.

"Is this the downside of linked litter-mates? Our defenses are linked to the point we can all be taken down if one is removed?" David asked. "Rese said he passed out during a mission when Rone almost died but he never said how long he was out of it."

Jackie's heart squeezed as she thought of them being in danger because of her. "I don't want anything to happen to any of you. How do we fix this? If we destroy this place will that fix it?"

"I doubt the place is what brought us here," David said. The next moment the small den disappeared and the four of them stood in a circle looking at each other. "It's our links. We're a part of each other."

"Can our links be changed so that this doesn't happen?" Jackie said thinking fast.

"I don't know," David said.

"Quinn and I were together when I got hurt, now I'm dead weight to him, unable to protect myself. What's the purpose of learning to fight and using someone else's energy if it could put me in a damn coma like this?" Frustration rolled through her. Years of training to learn to protect herself, gone, only to fall victim of something she had no control over.

"Can we break our links?" Adam said into the silence.

Jackie jerked around to face him. "What do you mean?"

"Break our connection." He looked at her, then David and finally Renee whose eyes had grown large.

"No. Just think of something else," Renee said wrapping her arms around her waist.

"Like what?" Adam said.

Renee shrugged. "I can't imagine life without you guys. You've always been a thought away no matter what, I need that." She looked at Jackie and released a long breath. "Sorry this is a problem for you and Quinn but breaking our link isn't the answer. The benefits outweigh this one problem. Maybe we can tone it down or something."

"This one problem can get us killed. Have you thought of that?" Adam asked her. "I thought I was dying when the pain from Jackie's wound slammed into me. If I'd been driving I could've gone off the road, hit someone else, who knows."

"You weren't dying, Adam. I was," Jackie said in a low voice, puzzling through everything. "We haven't fully completed our bonding. Maybe once Quinn and I do that, this won't happen again, at least from my end." She prayed what she said was true.

"I didn't mean it the way it sounded, Jackie," Adam said quickly. "It's just this whole one for all thing isn't as great as I thought it was. None of us realized our links could hold us captive like this."

"Most great benefits have side effects, the pendulum swings both ways. We've never been on this side of the swing before," David said. "I don't think there's anything we can do to change or fix our connection, it's too ingrained. Whatever we're dealing with now will weaken and release us soon. How do we want to handle it from now on?" He looked at Renee. "I don't think hiding something like this from Daddy is a good idea."

Renee groaned. "He's never going to let me go skiing again."

"You've never been skiing," Adam said.

"It's on my bucket list," Renee snapped her eyes shooting daggers at him.

Adam raised his hands and mimicked zipping his lips.

"You'll need to explain this to Quinn," David told Jackie. "But because of the danger it places the four of us in, ask him not to share the information."

Relieved they were coming up with some sort of plan, Jackie nodded. "Each of us will tell our mates before bonding so they understand the possibilities of passing out and the strength of our link. Like I said, once fully mated this may not happen again but it's better for them to be prepared if we go into a coma-like state." Quinn was probably already distraught thinking she was hurt. She prayed whatever held the four of them in stasis broke soon.

"Should I still go to Europe?" Adam asked in a somber tone. "Knowing I could be targeted because of Daddy hadn't really bothered me before. We trained for that most of our lives. With our energies combined I always knew I could fight my way out of any situation and win. Got to admit I felt invincible for a while knowing how hard it would be to take me out. But seeing this, the downside of fighting for my life." He shook his head. "With Rese and Rone, it's just two targets. With us, it's four. Any one of us could be the downfall of the others and I don't want to do that to you guys."

"None of us should stop living," Jackie said with a strong conviction and the knowledge she would continue to fight against rebels. "You've been playing sports before you could walk. We'll make this work, we always do. If you need my energy to heal, or fight, I'm here for you. Accidents are a part of life."

"Notice she said accidents," Renee said dryly. "Don't do crazy stuff without thinking about us." She laughed at the finger he showed her.

"Do we tell the parents?" David asked.

Jackie looked at him. No matter his feelings he would go along with the majority. They'd always been that way.

"Not yet," Adam said. "Renee made a good point. I'm ready to leave the compound, see some of the world." He looked at them. "I promise to be more careful now that I know what can happen. I swear I won't tell anyone about our Achilles heel, not even my mate until she accepts me. But I need to get away for a bit, I hope you guys trust me enough to allow that."

Jackie. 'Quinn's voice sounded like whispery wave she grabbed for their link with both hands.

Profound relief swamped her at the sound of his voice. *Quinn,"* she called.

Johnson's dead..." She caught bits and pieces of his sentence.

"One second guys, I hear Quinn," Jackie told them holding up a finger. "*Quinn, I'm here with my litter-mates.*"

I'don't understand.... Litter-mates...coming..." Quinn's words were breaking.

I'was hurt and my brothers and Renee helped me heal. Now we're stuck. Never mind I'll tell you later." She glanced at her siblings.

Your father... does he know? ....talking about?" Quinn said.

Jackie gritted her teeth at the bad connection. She wanted to put his mind at ease. "*No, the four of us, we have a quiet place we go.* 'She repeated that twice hoping he'd pick up on it. *Almost done. Almost done,*" she repeated so he'd understand she was returning to him soon. She couldn't make out his next words and then there was nothing. Where'd he go?

Quinn? Quinn? 'She called his name a few more times before realizing he left their link.

"You talked to him?" Renee asked when Jackie faced her.

"Some, it was a really bad connection. I got bits and pieces. Maybe I'll be awake soon." She offered a silent prayer to the Goddess to make this happen. Quinn leaving their link wasn't a good thing. She needed to know what was going on. *Please keep him safe,*" she prayed.

"Renee and Adam don't want to tell the parents of the dangers we face individually or collectively. Bear in mind how long we've been in this coma-like, or paralyzed state and think how Mama would feel if she walked into my or Adam's room right now and couldn't wake us," David said.

"That's not fair," Renee said turning to face David.

He shrugged without taking his gaze off Jackie.

"Daddy will make Jackie and Quinn come to the compound for tests to see if Quinn is the problem instead of us. You know how he gets," Renee said. "This whole passing out thing will become his new mission. I want to live my life free of more years beneath the microscope on how breeds function."

"I heard that," Adam said raising his fist. Renee touched his fist with her own before looking at Jackie.

Jackie agreed with Adam and Renee but didn't say it immediately. Instead she focused on David's comments. "Your points are valid, David. Mama would be upset if she couldn't wake you. She'd be concerned about the downside to us being linked. Keep in mind there are probably more downsides that we haven't triggered and won't know about until something happens. We wouldn't have known about this if I wasn't investigating rebels."

"What?" David said watching her closely.

"Rebels? Why?" Adam asked.

Jackie waved her hand. "That's not the point. What's important is I'm finally doing something that matters a lot to me and I don't want to stop for tests to learn what else happens through our connections. I love you guys and for better or worse we're linked in a weird way that defies understanding. I suggest we deal with each new challenge as it comes along. I'll talk to Quinn; explain our quad so he'll know what's happening." She paused. "I guess we'll need a wingman or a person or someone to watch our backs who's loyal." She shrugged. "We can keep this from Mama and Daddy for now, but not for long." She glanced at David before looking at Renee and Adam. "If they don't find out before, then we tell them next New Year's Day."

David nodded. "Agreed." He looked at them. "Take good care of yourselves and watch your backs. Daddy's calling me." He disappeared.

Jackie woke to Quinn lying next to her in the bed. She breathed in his scent, allowed it to fill her with peace and prayed he would understand her link to her siblings.

"Don't leave me," Quinn murmured in his sleep.

"Never," Jackie promised and brushed a kiss against the top of his head.

CHAPTER TWENTY-SIX

Three Days Later:

Jackie and Quinn stood behind the glass and watched Kristin's interrogation. Seated next to her attorney, her arrogant mask slipped as the District Attorney opened a file and pulled out the information regarding Kristin's hidden bank account. Her arrogance disappeared completely when the more damning videos of Kristin and Johnson discussing their deeds against Bradley were played.

Not only did Kristin not know her partner in crime was dual-natured, she also didn't realize the man taped their clandestine meetings and phone calls. Aaron Johnson proved to be a sneaky bitch who kept meticulous records.

Once Jackie and Quinn broke into Johnson's home, she found his safe with documentation of his nefarious activities. He'd never enrolled in the Nation's database and she hadn't found information regarding a den, litter, or anything from his past. He'd truly been a lone wolf living in the city. Jackie wondered if he was the money behind the rebels but found nothing to indicate he worked with rebels or anyone else.

The past two days Jackie worked feverishly using Bradley's restored documents from the cloud files and Johnson's records to put the finishing touches on a solid case against Kristin Cross. When all the pieces were in place Jackie met with the District Attorney to discuss her findings.

With Bradley and Johnson dead, Kristin was their only lead to Jonas. In exchange for the file on Kristin the District Attorney agreed to seek information from Kristin regarding Jonas' whereabouts. They waited for Kristin to tell them where Jonas was hiding.

"I told you his name is Jonas Gray but I haven't heard or seen him since the day of Mr. Bradley's death. I've been trying to find him but he's not answering my calls." She looked at her attorney. "Honestly, I don't know where he is. If I did I'd tell you. He's a bastard, the way he killed Aaron and Mr. Bradley." Eyes filled with tears, she looked at the District Attorney, a tough old bird in her early 60s. "I swear I had nothing to do with anybody dying."

"Just robbing their company?" the District Attorney asked.

"Don't answer that," Kristin's attorney said.

"We took a little here and there," Kristin hedged looking at the table.

"I have your bank records here," the District Attorney said. "It's a lot more than here and there I assure you."

Kristin nodded but didn't immediately respond. "Aaron had been doing it for years. When we started dating, he brought me in on it."

The District Attorney nodded. "How long did the two of you date?" The way she said "date" made it clear what she thought really happened.

"Three years, on and off," Kristin said, glancing at her attorney and then back at the District Attorney.

Jackie sent the District Attorney a text message. "Did she call Bradley the day he died?" The phone and everything in the house had been destroyed in the fire and since it was a throw-away phone they had no way to check incoming calls.

When asked, Kristin's eyes widened slightly. She sat back in her chair and crossed her leg. "No, I didn't talk to him that day. We talked briefly the night before, he wasn't feeling well."

"She's lying," Jackie said.

Quinn wrapped his arm around her pulling her close. He rubbed his chin against her scalp, calming her. "She's going to prison for a very long time. Just think, she'll never spend any of the money she stole, all of that, for nothing."

"It was a gamble and she lost," Jackie agreed. Still, it pissed her off Kristin wouldn't pay for Mr. Bradley's death. They'd been unable to tie the woman to the explosion and had to settle with putting her behind bars for a considerable portion of her life on multiple counts of fraud.

The District Attorney glanced at the glass and asked another question. Kristin looked at the glass and frowned. As much as Jackie wanted to punch the woman in the face, anonymity was the one thing the District Attorney insisted on.

"Let's go," Quinn said moving toward the door. "It's too hot and humid in this city. Your parents are expecting us."

Jackie nodded and walked out with him in silence. They hadn't learned anything new about Taurus' whereabouts but her father sent his picture to all the Alphas, KnightForce and the Knights with instructions to find him.

After speaking with Penny and Marsha, her dad declared Jonas or Taurus an enemy of the Nation which was akin to a death warrant, except he wanted the full-blood alive. Jonas' days of walking in the light among humans were over. In Jackie's mind it couldn't have happened to a nicer guy, she just hoped they found him soon. For now, she had to be satisfied with what she and Quinn had done to bring about justice for Mr. Bradley.

When she'd come out of her comatose state in the hospital, Quinn had been happy, relieved and later told her how jealous he'd felt thinking she chose her siblings over him. His confession opened the door for their conversation regarding the link with her litter-mates. It had been long six hours, filled with questions and what it meant for them.

"So if you pass out in the middle of sex, it may not be my amazing skills," Quinn had asked.

"Who knows, it could be." Glad he accepted her quirks and all she had hugged him close. That night they finished mating.

The next day they teleconferenced with Ramos and Antwan who wanted Quinn to run the clinic Alpha Gilbert offered to build at the ranch. Jackie wasn't keen on the idea of living in Tennessee; she'd left home to see more of the world and to make a difference. Quinn told Ramos he and Jackie would be traveling before settling in one place but agreed to look over any plans before construction.

"*Alpha Theron sent a car to take us to the jetport, we should be at the compound in time for dinner,*" Jackie said as they left the government building and veered toward the charcoal gray SUV.

"*So, are we really saying goodbye to Houston? You don't have to give it all up if you're not ready.*" He slid in the back seat next to her.

Over the past few days, going through all the files, seeing the greed and duplicity sickened Jackie to the point she swore off the city. In calmer moments, she realized her disgust was with particular individuals and not the town. *Maybe. I told Alpha Theron I'd let him know in a month or so if we want to sell the house and car. I love that car,* 'she said wistfully.

We can take it to Tennessee, leave it there for when we visit the ranch. That way we'll have two vehicles there, 'Quinn said.

"*That sounds good.*" Jackie and Nionis planned to get together whenever she returned to Tennessee, it'd be good to have her own car to come and go as she chose. Snuggling close to Quinn, Jackie took his hand in hers and kissed the back of it. "*Nervous?*"

"*To meet your sire and mam?*"

Grinning, she nodded.

"*No. Spoke to them both and look forward to planning our mating celebration.*"

You've been talking to Renee, 'she accused.

He nodded. *She's got me thinking a wedding isn't a bad idea.*"

Jackie groaned. "Don't forget I'm the bride and I'm not sure I want all that."

He squeezed her shoulder and kissed her forehead. "I want whatever you want."

Smiling, Jackie snuggled closer as they headed toward the plane.

Several hours later, Jackie walked into her mom's outstretched arms and received a warm, loving hug. "Mama, I missed you," Jackie said breathing in her mom's scent.

Jasmine placed a kiss on Jackie's cheek and turned to Quinn. "I missed you too, sweetie."

Without moving from her mom's embrace, Jackie extended her hand to Quinn who took it and moved closer. "Mama this is Quinn York, my mate. I'm a lucky girl to have him," she added winking at Quinn who shook his head at her.

"I'm lucky." He bent forward and brushed a kiss against her forehead.

"I'm Jasmine." She smiled and wrapped her arm around his waist. "Welcome to my home and our family." She looked at Jackie staring up at her mate and then at Quinn whose smoldering gaze lingered on Jackie's mouth.

"I'd say both of you are blessed to have each other. Let's have a seat. Silas and Angus are on their way," Jasmine said moving further into the living room.

Holding hands, Jackie and Quinn sat on the love seat, grinning and leaning into each other. When Silas and Angus entered the room they stopped next to Jasmine who remained standing watching the young couple.

"I don't think they know we're here," Jasmine told Silas. *"Were we like that? I don't recall."*

"We're like that now," Silas said taking her hand and kissing the back of it. *"You're all I see when I enter a room."*

She chuckled. *"Good try."* She accepted a hug from Angus and stood between the two men.

"So, you're the pup mated to my niece," Angus said.

Quinn and Jackie looked at them and blinked. Jackie bolted from her seat with her arms outstretched to Angus who hugged her close. Quinn stood, stuffed his hands in his pockets and moved closer to his mate while glancing at the two men. He waited until Jackie hugged her sire and stepped back taking his hand. "Daddy you've linked with Quinn already. Uncle Angus this is Quinn York my mate," Jackie said moving from foot to foot with a wide grin.

Jasmine watched her normally serious daughter laugh with abandon at something Angus said without ever releasing her mate's hand. *"She's really happy,"* she told Silas.

"Seems so."

"She seems more relaxed, balanced."

"Mating does that to you," Silas said watching Quinn and Jackie interact with Angus.

"You'll meet my mate and pups tonight at dinner." Angus looked at Jasmine. "He'll meet everyone tonight, right?"

"Yes, we're having a family dinner. I think Nionis flew in for moral support or to give Cameron an update of her recent activities," Jasmine said.

Jackie faced Quinn. *"My brothers are leaving soon so I wanted you to meet them. Mom opened dinner to everybody so we get it out the way all at once. It won't be bad, I promise. You'll get used to a large family."* She leaned into him.

Quinn's arm tightened around her waist as he rubbed his chin against her forehead. His gaze met Jasmine's and she nodded with a teary smile.

"Jackie Knight, I love you and nothing else matters. It's an honor to meet those who loved and nurtured you as you grew up," he said.

Jackie leaned back, pulled him close and kissed him.

"Well, I suppose we're keeping him," Silas told Jasmine sounding unhappy.

"Yes, she's in love with him and he's in love with her and will make her happy. That's all I want for all of them," Jasmine said waving good-bye to Angus.

"Happy is a good starting point, I'd like a little more." Silas paused. *"But this one works well for our Jackie, they're a good match."*

Jasmine mimicked her daughter and pulled Silas in for a searing kiss.

Hello,

I love paranormal books and characters in general and shifter stories in particular. Throw in the romantic element, strong Alpha characters who bend beneath the power of love and I'm over the moon. Sighs…

Thank you for taking the time to read Jackie's Journey, Book one in La Patron's Den. Jackie's a strong, intelligent woman with a strong sense of loyalty and a high moral compass. If Quinn hadn't been her mate would she have turned him in for disobeying the law? Maybe. Being able to see both sides of a coin is an excellent trait and one that serves this puzzle-fixing, serious pup. Just as family is important to Jasmine, she's taught and demonstrated that love to her children. And although their bonds are tested, so far they haven't broken. But then again, we haven't read Adam's story, which is next.

You're invited to journey with me through all the books in this series. If you like fast paced action, suspense and great love connections like me, you won't be disappointed. Feel free to drop me a line, SydneyAddae@msn.com or join my Facebook group, La Patron's Den, where discussions regarding Silas and the Wolf nation abound. Also you can find me at my website, SydneyAddae.com.

Knight Chronicles is a newsletter for my Readers Group from the characters of the series to keep you informed of what's going on in the Wolf Nation. Each issue has a personal message from Silas Knight, La Patron, or his mate, Jasmine. Character profiles with in-depth interviews and thoughts you won't find anywhere else. Also works in progress, new releases and special give-aways in every issue. If you would like to receive **Knight Chronicles** click this sign up link! Thank you. (http://eepurl.com/bb3csz)

La Patron, the Alpha's Alpha is my first paranormal series and I'd like to ask a favor. When you finish reading, **please leave a review**, whatever your opinion, I assure you I appreciate it.

Thanks again
Sydney

BirthRight
BirthControl
BirthMark
BirthStone
BirthDate
BirthSign
Sword of Inquest
Sword of Mercy
Sword of Justice
La Patron's Christmas
La Patron's Christmas 2
La Patron's New Year – w/Catherine Marsh, & Leigh West
KnightForce 1
KnightForce Deuces
KnightForce Tres'
KnightForce Damian
KnightForce Ethan
Angus
La Patron's Den – Jackie's Journey
La Patron's Den - Awakening the Alpha, Adam

Booksets
La Patron Series Books 1-6
La Patron Series Books 4-6
La Patron's Sword

Vampires:
Last in Line

Bear:
Bear With Me
Jewel's Bear

www.ingramcontent.com/pod-product-compliance
Lightning Source LLC
Chambersburg PA
CBHW070501260626
47161CB00004B/1403